SIX HOURS AWAY

RETURN TO LIGHTHOUSE POINT

KAY CORRELL

ZURA LU PUBLISHING, LLC

Published by Zura Lu Publishing LLC

091720

This book is dedicated to my reader group on Facebook.

You guys are the best! So supportive. Always there for me.

I couldn't do this without you.

You have my deepest gratitude.

KAY'S BOOKS

Find more information on all my books at *kaycorrell.com*

COMFORT CROSSING ~ THE SERIES

The Shop on Main - Book One
The Memory Box - Book Two
The Christmas Cottage - A Holiday Novella (Book 2.5)
The Letter - Book Three
The Christmas Scarf - A Holiday Novella (Book 3.5)
The Magnolia Cafe - Book Four
The Unexpected Wedding - Book Five

The Wedding in the Grove - (a crossover short

story between series - with Josephine and Paul from The Letter.)

LIGHTHOUSE POINT ~ THE SERIES

Wish Upon a Shell - Book One
Wedding on the Beach - Book Two
Love at the Lighthouse - Book Three
Cottage near the Point - Book Four
Return to the Island - Book Five
Bungalow by the Bay - Book Six

CHARMING INN ~ Return to Lighthouse Point

One Simple Wish - Book One
Two of a Kind - Book Two
Three Little Things - Book Three
Four Short Weeks - Book Four
Five Years or So - Book Five
Six Hours Away - Book Six
Charming Christmas - Book Seven

SWEET RIVER ~ THE SERIES

A Dream to Believe in - Book One
A Memory to Cherish - Book Two
A Song to Remember - Book Three
A Time to Forgive - Book Four
A Summer of Secrets - Book Five

A Moment in the Moonlight - Book Six

INDIGO BAY ~ A multi-author sweet romance series

Sweet Days by the Bay - Kay's Complete Collection of stories in the Indigo Bay series

Or buy them separately:

Sweet Sunrise - Book Three
Sweet Holiday Memories - A short holiday story
Sweet Starlight - Book Nine

Sign up for my newsletter at my website *kaycorrell.com* to make sure you don't miss any new releases or sales.

CHAPTER 1

Lillian looked at the long list of storm preparations scratched onto the crinkled paper on her desk. Even with help, she'd only managed to make a small dent in them so far today.

More hurricane shutters needed to be put up at Charming Inn. They had a good supply of bottled water and a generator to keep the fridge and freezer going if the electricity went out. They'd gotten extra gas for the generator. She got to check that off her list.

She always kept a supply of candles and lanterns around, so that had been an easy check, too. But there were so, so many other things to do to get ready.

Hurricane season. It was always such a stressful time each year.

She clicked on the computer to check the forecast for the approaching storm. No change. It was still predicted to go north of them, though of course, they'd get strong winds and torrential rain.

She took a deep breath to steady her nerves. The work would all get done. It always did.

She looked up to see Gary standing in the doorway to her office, watching her. Her heart did a quick double beat. She wasn't quite used to the feeling that rushed through her when she saw him.

Her husband. She glanced down at the ring on her finger. They'd been married less than twenty-four hours. Who knew that all this storm preparation would be how they'd spend their first day as husband and wife?

"How long have you been standing there?"

"Not long. Just watching... my wife." His eyes twinkled and his mouth curved into a smile. "My wife. I like the sound of that."

The heat of a blush crept across her face. "Oh, go on."

He entered the room. "So, where do you want me next? I thought I could get the rest of the shutters up on the beachside of the inn. Jay said he'd help after he gets things settled in the kitchen."

"That would be great."

"Then I'll put shutters on The Nest."

Lillian smiled. The Nest, her private area of the inn where she and her niece, Sara, had lived. Until Sara had married and moved out, and now Gary had moved in as of last night.

"Leave the one off the kitchen window for now. It's quick and easy to put up, and I like some light coming in. And we'll pull the folding shutter across the doors to the deck when the storm gets closer, though I have that one hurricane door I put in last year when I needed to replace a slider, so we'll still be able to see out there, too."

"Sure thing." Gary shook his head. "Who knew it was so much work to protect against a hurricane that might not even come very close?"

"It's the unpredictability of the storms that gets us. We've pretty much perfected the whole getting-ready-for-a-storm routine." She shrugged. "And we always hope it passes around us and all the preparations were for nothing."

"Better to be too prepared than not ready."

"The guests have been notified and most are packing up to leave. I've sent emails out to guests who were scheduled to arrive later this week and next, explaining the forecast, and offering refunds or to rebook for a later date. I'm having the front desk person make calls to all incoming guests, too. There's not an evacuation order, but we can't handle an inn full of guests if the electricity goes out. I always err on the side of safety when a storm is predicted to be this strong."

"I don't know how you juggle all this, but you're doing a great job. I'm impressed."

Her heart swelled at the compliment. Gary walked over and kissed her forehead, just a simple gesture between a married couple, but one that meant the world to her. Her heart fluttered again. *How did I get so lucky?* She hoped he always made her feel this way.

Gary turned to leave. "I'm going to get back to work. Let me know if you need me for anything."

"Thank you, again, for delaying the honeymoon so I could stay and get the inn ready."

"Don't you know by now that I'd do

anything for you?" He gave her a quick smile and disappeared out the door.

Her heart did that little flip yet again. She'd married a very good man.

ZOE BIRCH HEADED to the community center to help her uncle, Noah. He ran the center and was busy getting it ready for the storm. If the storm got stronger or was predicted to come closer, the community center would be used as a place where people could go to ride things out.

The center had been built to strict standards to—*technically*—sustain the high winds of strong hurricanes. Though luckily it hadn't ever been fully tested. But people in older homes on the island would often come and wait out the storm at the center, whether in an effort to remain safer or for the companionship, Zoe was never sure.

She hurried down the sidewalk, waving at a few people putting up shutters. The grocery store was packed with people stocking up. She remembered the drill from growing up on the island. Bottled water, batteries, candles, food that didn't need to be cooked in case the electricity went out.

They'd had a few fairly big storms come through in the years she'd lived here, but luckily none had done much damage to the town or their home. Though one time a storm had taken out the electricity to the whole island. It was out eight long days in the suffocating heat of late August. She remembered every detail of that storm. Noah had taken her to the beach to swim each day in an effort to beat the heat, but by the time they walked back to their house, they'd be sweltering again. She hoped the electricity stayed on this time. She wasn't anxious to repeat the eight-day outage.

It was strange to think that just yesterday she'd been celebrating Lillian and Gary's wedding. And it had been wonderful. A beautiful ceremony and a fun reception in spite of the threat of the storm this week.

She'd been sorry to see Gary's son, Mason, leave to head back to his home in Seattle this morning, but it was the sensible decision to get out of town before the storm hit. She'd thoroughly enjoyed her outings with Mason this past week and their time together at the wedding. She smiled, recalling how they'd danced the night away with Mason holding her close. She also vividly remembered the kiss he'd given her before he'd left town this morning.

She pushed the thoughts away as she hurried down the sidewalk to the center. She'd keep busy helping Noah get the center ready. That was better than feeling sorry for herself that Mason was gone. She didn't even know if she'd ever see him again unless they both just happened to be back on the island at the same time.

Just her luck. Fall for a man who lived a six-hour flight away from her.

She pushed into the center and went to find Noah. She found him in the back storage room, dragging out the hurricane shutters.

"I've come to help." She walked over to him.

"Don't you think you should head back home?" Noah's forehead creased in a frown.

"The roads are already jammed with people leaving the area. I thought I'd stay here. Especially since the storm is predicted to hit north of here. It's probably safer here than up north."

Noah nodded. "You're probably right. I hate to think of you spending half the day stuck in traffic on a trip that usually takes a couple hours at most."

"Well, I've come to help. The shutters are numbered, right? Start at the front corner?"

"You act like you've done this a time or two." He grinned. "You get started on those, and I'm going to drag more tables and chairs out to the main room. Need to check on the bottled water supply here, too. Though, people are pretty good about bringing water and food with them when they come."

"Hand me the drill with the wing nut screwer-on-thingie attachment. I'm not screwing those suckers on by hand."

He smiled at her description and handed her the drill. She grabbed the next shutter and went outside. The clear blue sky and white clouds mocked all the townspeople scurrying around with preparations.

She put up the first shutter, then another. The heat of the day weighed down on her as she struggled to put each shutter on. She shoved damp wisps of hair back from her face, still fighting with a particularly obstinate shutter.

"Hey, you."

She whirled around at the sound of the familiar voice.

Mason. Her pulse raced and delight bubbled through her.

"Mason. What are you doing here? You just left."

He helped her adjust a shutter into place and held it up for her. "About that. I decided I should really stay here and help Lillian and Dad with the inn. They'll be short-handed and there's so much work to be done to close it up. I think I'm needed here more than back home in the boardroom." He tossed her that half-smile of his and his one dimple deepened.

"I'm sure they can use your help." And yet, he was here with her, not at the inn.

"When I got to the inn, Lillian sent me over here to help with the community center. She said if it gets worse, the center will house a lot of the townspeople."

"Yes... I... well..." She sounded like a fool. *Pull it together.* "Noah will be glad for the help."

"Good."

He'd changed from his usual attire of dress slacks and collared shirt into shorts and a t-shirt. The shirt stretched across his chest and tapered down to his waist. He'd finished his outfit with sturdy looking sandals. She realized she'd been staring at him, and he tossed her yet another lazy grin.

That grin was her downfall.

She tried to still her pounding heart as he held the shutter and she used the drill to screw on a wing nut holding the shutter in place, then another one.

They fell into a routine and worked side by side for hours putting up the shutters until she swore she couldn't raise her arms again.

Noah came around to the far side of the community center. She and Mason had gotten shutters up on all but the front.

"Mason, what are you doing here?" Noah reached out a hand.

Mason wiped his hand on his shorts, then reached out and shook Noah's hand. "Decided to come back and help. It seemed silly and selfish to just dodge out of town with the storm coming and work needing to be done. I knew Lillian could use help, but she sent me over here. Said you might have a lot of people here if the storm got bad and she wanted to make sure it was ready."

"Typical Lil, always worrying about others." Noah looked down the side of the building. "I was wondering how Zoe had gotten so many shutters up. Appreciate your help, Mason." Noah turned to her. "You look tired. And I was thinking. You should move out of the inn and back to our house."

Since Noah and Lillian's niece, Sara, were newlyweds, she'd been staying at Charming Inn this week instead of with her uncle. She'd wanted to give them their privacy.

Okay, and she'd enjoyed staying at the inn where Mason was staying. That, too.

"You know, Uncle Noah, I think I'll just stay at my room in the inn. I can help out Lillian that way. But I'll come back to the center to help you too." And Mason would be staying at the inn again...

Noah frowned. "I'd feel better if you came back home."

"Uncle Noah, I'll be fine. And I can help at the inn."

"I suppose so." Noah looked from her to Mason and back to her, then a brief smile crossed his lips. "Okay, but why don't you two call it a day? We can finish up the shutters tomorrow. Go get cleaned up and something to eat. I'm going to track down Sara."

"She was at the inn helping Lillian earlier," Mason chimed in as he handed the drill to

Noah and turned to her. "Come on. Let's go back to the inn."

And suddenly she was walking down the sidewalk with Mason… something she'd never imagined would be happening when he'd said goodbye to her this morning.

And when he had kissed her this morning.

A kiss she swore she could still feel on her lips.

CHAPTER 2

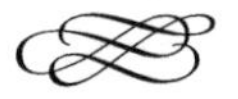

Robin appreciated the help of her best friends, Sara and Charlotte, as they dragged beach chairs and umbrellas in from the beach at the inn and put them into storage. The three friends talked and laughed as they helped each other. Everyone pitched in when a storm was coming.

They finally finished and went to the deck at The Nest, exhausted, and sat and sipped some sweet tea.

Robin kicked off her sandals and propped her feet up on a lower railing. "That was a long day." This was the first big storm to head their direction—or kind of their direction—since she'd agreed to become a manager of the inn with Lillian. She really should keep chipping away at the to-do list, but she just needed a quick five-minute break.

Charlotte leaned back and propped up her feet, too. "I don't care if I ever see another beach chair."

Sara laughed. "But after the storm, all those chairs and umbrellas will need to go back out."

"I guess so, won't they? We must have made a million trips across the beach." Charlotte took a sip of her tea. "And I will come back and help then. But for now, I'm just going to rest for a few minutes, then I'll head to the marina and check on Ben. Last I heard he was busy securing boats as best they could. And people were dropping off their boats for storage there on the lot, too."

"How does one secure one of those huge boats?" Robin asked.

"I have no clue. But Ben does."

"I hope the whole thing just goes around us. Or weakens." Sara shook her head. "I love being back in Florida, but I'd forgotten how much work storm prep was."

Robin frowned as she looked up the hurricane forecast on her phone. "Well, that's not good news."

"What?" Sara's eyebrow rose.

"The storm has gotten a bit stronger. Still a tropical storm, though, not a hurricane. Yet."

"Still predicted to hit north of here?" Charlotte frowned.

"So far."

Robin took a last sip of her tea and let out a long sigh. "I should get back to work."

Charlotte stood. "And I should go to the marina. *And* we still need to finish getting the shutters up on the bungalow."

"Jay helped me get some of them up earlier today. Let me check on things here, then I'll meet you back at the bungalow and we'll finish those," Robin said. Just another thing on the long list of things to do.

"I'm going to find Noah and see where he needs me. Shuttering the house, or prepping the community center." Sara stood. "Here, hand me your glasses. I'll get these washed up."

Robin hurried off through the inn. She found Jay in the kitchen wearing one of his ever-present t-shirts. This one proclaimed—*Dinner provided with a side of sarcasm.* He flashed her a smile as she entered. He held out his arms, and she walked into his embrace. He held her close for a moment before letting her go. "You doing okay?"

She smiled up at him. "I am now."

"We put out sandwiches for the few guests who are still here. Some are leaving early morning."

Dana, the assistant cook, walked into the kitchen and up to them. Robin scooted away from Jay. No one even knew they were a couple yet.

If Dana had noticed how close they'd been standing, she didn't say anything. "Jay, why don't you go? I'll get things cleaned up after the sandwiches are gone. And I have another batch of sourdough bread rising that's almost ready to bake. I'll bake that up, then head out."

"You sure?" Jay asked.

"Yep."

"Let's go." Jay led Robin out of the kitchen. "So, where do you need my help?"

"I need to check with Lillian, but if there's nothing pressing here, I need to finish getting shutters up on the bungalow."

"I'm your man."

"You are?" She grinned, still not used to the fact that after five years they'd finally gotten together as a couple. It was all still so new. "I'll meet you in the lobby in about fifteen minutes?"

"I'll be there."

She went to find Lillian, a small smile on her face, still feeling the warmth of his hug.

ROBIN AND JAY worked side by side, finishing putting up the shutters on the bungalow. If she never screwed on another shutter it would be too soon.

"I can finish them. Why don't you go inside? You look beat." Jay took the shutter from her hands.

"I can't let you do that."

"Of course you can. How about you go in and make us some iced tea? It won't take me long to finish these last few windows."

She was too tired to argue with him. She went inside and looked in the fridge. Luckily Charlotte had made a big pitcher of sweet tea. Perfect. She washed up at the sink, though she really craved a cool shower. She poured them tall glasses of tea, and as she sat down at the table—so thankful to finally be off her feet—Jay came inside.

"All finished."

He washed his hands at the sink, then dropped onto a chair across from her.

Robin pushed his glass across the table. He took a large gulp of tea and slid the back of his hand across his mouth.

"Thirsty?" she teased.

"Yes. Very. It appears this storm prep is thirsty business."

"Robin? You here?" Charlotte called out as she entered the bungalow.

"In the kitchen."

Charlotte walked into the kitchen. "You got the shutters all up without me."

"Jay helped."

Charlotte turned to Jay. "Well, thanks. I think you're my favorite person. After dragging the beach chairs and umbrellas in and helping Ben at the marina, I'm about done in. Now that I'm back here on the island, I remember how much I detest storm prep. I think I'm just going to head to bed. *After* a nice long shower. It's so muggy out there."

"It is." Robin nodded. "Well, good night. See you in the morning."

"Night." Charlotte disappeared down the hallway.

Jay leaned back in his seat and eyed her. "So... we're still going to have that official real first date, right?"

"Sure. But it will have to wait until after the storm."

"Have you told Charlotte or Sara about... us?"

"Not yet. It's just... so new. I was going to tell them while we were working on bringing all the beach things in at the inn, but... well, we were talking about the storm and Lillian's wedding and..." She shrugged. "I didn't know what to say. Hey guys, Jay kissed me. I think we're a couple now?"

He tossed a lazy grin at her. "Something like that."

"It's not that I care if people know... it's just..."

He reached across the table and covered her hand. "It's okay. It's a lot all at once, isn't it? We can wait to tell people."

"You keep pulling me into your arms like you did in the kitchen and everyone will figure it out." She turned her hand over and laced her fingers through his.

"I'm pretty sure Dana has it figured out." Jay nodded. "But I don't care who knows it. I want everyone to know it. Robin Baker is my girl."

"Your girl?" She tilted her head.

"I don't know the proper thing to call it. My girlfriend? My significant other?"

"You can call me whatever you want."

"How about if I call you the woman I love?" He stood up, came around the table, and pulled her to her feet. "And I'd like to kiss that woman."

"That sounds like a practical idea." She nodded soberly, hiding a smile.

"I'm nothing if not practical." He leaned down and kissed her.

She slipped her arms around his waist and pulled him close, never wanting to let him go.

CHAPTER 3

Mason and Zoe grabbed sandwiches when they got back to the inn.

"I managed to snag a couple bottles of wine on my way back into town. Want to eat on the balcony of my room and have some wine?" Mason offered. "I got my same room again. I'm right next to yours."

She quickly hid a delighted smile. He'd be close. Right next door to her. And honestly, with an almost empty inn, she'd like having him close. That was all it was—the fact the inn was almost empty. The thought rang a bit false even as she tried to convince herself.

"That sounds good. But would you mind if I grab a quick shower first?" She knew she must look like a bedraggled cat after all the exertion of putting up the shutters.

"No, that sounds like a good idea. Could use one myself. So, say twenty minutes? Oh, wait. Is that enough time?" He laughed. "I have no clue if that's enough time for you. Women take more time to get ready, right?"

Zoe smiled. "That's plenty of time for me." She hurried into her room and took a cooling shower, washing away the heat and grime of the day. She grabbed a clean pair of shorts and one of her favorite t-shirts. The blow-dryer sounded too hot and like too much work, so she'd let her hair dry on its own.

She headed to Mason's room, and he opened the door immediately when she knocked. He stood there in clean khaki shorts and a t-shirt stretched across his broad shoulders. His damp, precisely cut hair framed his temples, and his mouth broke into a welcoming smile. "There you are. Good. I'm famished. I set us up out on the balcony."

She followed him out onto the balcony, welcoming the breeze blowing in from the sea. She settled into a chair and he sat across from her.

He raised his glass. "For a job well done at the community center."

She clinked her glass with his, then took a sip. The wine was a delicious, full-bodied red, just like she liked. Had he remembered that from the few times they'd gone out? She set her glass down on the small cafe table.

"I was lucky to get this mini-suite again... though Lillian said most of the guests have checked out due to the storm. I like the room, though. There's a tiny kitchenette. A fridge that I filled with beer. There's a coffee pot, and I picked up some Sumatra coffee. You know. Essentials."

"Ah, essentials. Wine, beer, coffee."

"I also picked up nachos, pretzels, and apples." His face crinkled into a wry grin.

"But of course. More necessities." To be honest, with the great shape he was in, she would have pictured him more of a health food nut, following the newest healthy eating trend.

As they ate their dinner, she relaxed and enjoyed their easy banter. She liked that about being with Mason. It was easy. Comfortable. And yet, she could feel the underlying tension between them. Was he thinking about their kiss this morning as much as she was?

After they finished their meal, Mason took the dishes inside. They moved to a pair of Adirondack chairs and sat sipping their wine as the sun began to sink on the horizon.

"It's hard to imagine a storm is coming. It looks so peaceful out there." She stretched out her legs and slipped off her sandals.

"It does. I've never been through something like this. We don't get hurricanes in Seattle. Or tornados. Our big worry with natural disasters are earthquakes, but even those are usually mild."

"Hopefully this storm will stall at sea and weaken."

"So you know these are coming and you have days and days and days of just waiting and watching?"

"Pretty much."

"Ever get used to it?"

"Not really. But it's a reality we live with." She shrugged.

They finished their wine, and she stood. "I guess I should head back to my room."

"So soon?" He jumped up and stood beside her. "We could walk down to the shoreline. Watch the waves in the moonlight? I'm all... wound up."

Who could resist that impossibly impish grin? She hadn't wanted to overdo her stay with the invite to his room. But now *he* was suggesting a walk to the beach. Sounded perfect to her.

"I'm a bit wound up myself. It's always an uneasy time waiting on a storm. Let's go to the beach."

They walked down through the inn, across the deck, and out onto the beach. The stars were beginning to come out as the sky darkened, and the moon rolled its silvery beams down toward the beach.

He took her hand in his as they crossed the sand. She looked down at their interconnected hands then back up to find him staring at her. His eyes twinkled.

"You know what, Zoe Birch? I'm pretty darn happy I decided to stay on the island."

"You know what, Mason Jones? I am, too." A warm glow spread through her. Though, she did feel just the tiniest bit guilty at feeling this happy with the storm approaching and the work and chaos it was causing. But for now, for this moment, she was just going to enjoy being with Mason.

MASON STOOD on his balcony long after he'd walked Zoe back to her room. She'd unlocked her door and stood there, looking... beautiful. He really should have kissed her again.

Why hadn't he?

What a mistake. He'd certainly wanted to.

This morning's goodbye kiss had seemed... *appropriate*... due to the situation. They thought he was leaving and probably wouldn't see her again. But now he was on uneasy footing. It's not like they were officially dating or anything. If she lived in Seattle, it would be different. He would for sure be asking her out. Asking her out often. But now?

He stared out at the vast display of stars twinkling above him.

Now what?

He really enjoyed spending time with her. Even if it was just putting up hurricane shutters.

She'd looked beautiful in the moonlight tonight. Her hair had finally air-dried and drifted around her shoulders in the slight breeze. It had taken all his control to not just wrap her in his arms and kiss her. Run his fingers through that hair of hers.

He let out a long breath. This was why it was easier to just casually date women. That was so uncomplicated. This thing with Zoe —whatever it was—*that* was complicated.

He just wasn't sure about... anything. Wasn't sure of the timing. Wasn't sure how things actually stood between them.

The one thing he *was* sure about was he wasn't a man who liked feeling unsure.

CHAPTER 4

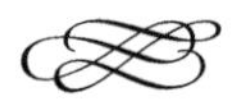

Robin found Jay in the kitchen at the inn early the next morning. Lillian was in the kitchen, too, so Jay just gave her a quick smile and a wink. A smile spread across her face. Her heart sang with delight, blissfully happy with the simple, shared smile.

"We've decided to just put out a buffet breakfast this morning for the few guests who are still here." Lillian lifted a tray of cinnamon rolls. "It's easier on everyone. We let all the guests know last night that all food would be buffet-style until after the storm." She headed out the door to the dining room.

Jay glanced toward the door where Lillian disappeared. He leaned down and before she knew it, he gave her a quick kiss. "Morning."

She loved the sound of his voice. The deep, sexy tones. The way that one word seemed to say so much.

"Morning." She reached up and touched his face, but then quickly brought her hand to her side, looking around the kitchen to see if anyone was watching.

His mouth curved into a smile. "So, did you come to swipe a cinnamon roll?"

"I did. And coffee. I so need coffee before I tackle this day."

"Come sit at the counter by me while I work and you inhale coffee."

She grabbed a roll and the coveted cup of coffee and went to sit next to him as he worked, frying up an immense amount of bacon. It was so nice to be back to being friends. She'd missed their chats in the kitchen while he worked. Well, she guessed they were more than friends now, but still friends. She watched as he scrambled up eggs and placed them in a large metal serving dish.

"Got to run this out to the buffet and put it on the warmer. Be right back."

She swiped a piece of bacon—then a second one—while she waited for him. Who could resist bacon?

Jay grinned when he came back in and saw her plate but didn't say anything. Dana came and grabbed some more flour for the bread she was making.

Lillian returned with a frown on her face. "Robin, did you take yesterday's deposit to the bank and drop it in the night deposit box?"

"I didn't take it to the bank, no."

Jay whirled around. "Is money missing again?"

Dana dropped the bag of flour on the counter. "Oh, sorry." She picked it up, looked at Lillian, then hurried back to her work station.

"Yes, there is. And I got that new safe with the new combination."

Jay turned to Dana. "Could you run this tray of cinnamon rolls out to the dining room? And check to make sure there's enough coffee."

Dana came over, got the tray, and left the kitchen.

"We don't need everyone knowing what's going on." Jay nodded in the direction Dana had gone, then held up his hands. "Not it. You never told me the new combination."

Lillian rolled her eyes. "Which is silly. Of course, I'd trust you with the combination, but I understand after Sheriff Dave accused you of stealing the money last week why you wouldn't want to know the new one."

"How is someone getting in there to get to the money?" Robin frowned.

"I don't know. I've even been locking my office door when I leave, along with locking the safe."

Jay turned back to Lillian and frowned. "We put in those keycard locks on the doors to the inn that lock at night so guests have to use a card to get in or out. How is someone getting into the inn?"

"I don't know." Lillian shrugged. "And I'm not going to call the sheriff again. Not after I told him the last missing money was found."

"Only it wasn't. You were just getting the sheriff to quit thinking I took it." Jay eyed her.

"Maybe we should put a video surveillance camera in the office?" Robin suggested.

"That's a good idea. I'll pick one up today and install it." Jay nodded.

"Let's keep this quiet. Not tell the staff. There's enough on everyone's minds with the storm." Lillian sighed. "And I just heard that they think the storm may hit as a category one hurricane now. So we'll get strong winds being on the edge of the storm. The forecast shows the storm going even more north of us right now. Let's hope it stays that way. Not that I wish ill on the coastline above us."

"I hope it does slip north of us," Jay said.

Robin slipped off the stool. "I should get to work."

"I'll catch you later." Jay smiled at her. That smile again.

Lillian left the kitchen as Dana came back in, her face creased in worry.

"Everything okay?"

Dana snapped her chin up. "Yes, just need to get more food out there. And the storm... it's making me a bit jumpy."

"They do that. It's all the waiting and watching to see what's going to happen."

Dana nodded in agreement, but still looked worried.

Robin hurried off to her office to see what was next on her long list of to-dos.

Zoe filled her plate—probably with too much food—but she was famished this morning. There was no resisting Jay's cinnamon rolls. She looked around at the few filled tables and saw Mason wave to her.

Her heart did a quick pitter-patter and she nodded at him, her hands full. He jumped up and came to help her, grabbing one of her plates. She was embarrassed she had two, but she'd seen the fresh fruit and had grabbed a small plate of that, too.

"I see you're up early today." Mason smiled but thankfully didn't mention all the food.

"Feeling a bit restless. And I wanted to see where I could help today." They headed over to Mason's table.

"Can I get you some coffee? Black, right?" he asked.

"Yes." She nodded. The man did remember the tiniest details about her. Like how she liked her coffee. She glanced over at the cup of coffee by his plate and saw it was black. She'd remember that now.

He brought the coffee and sat down across from her. "So, you heading to the community center to help?"

"I am."

"I asked Lillian if I could help her, but she said to go to the center again because if the storm does become a hurricane, lots of people will be taking shelter there. So I guess I'll be joining you helping out at the center today."

That suited her just fine. Not that the storm intensity was increasing, but that Mason would be spending the day with her.

She devoured her breakfast and topped it with another cup of coffee.

Mason sat across from her with an amused smile on his face.

"What are you smiling about?"

"Just watching you enjoy your breakfast."

She blushed. "I was hungry..."

He laughed. "Never understood women picking at their food or insisting on only eating salads with no dressing with an air of self-righteousness."

Well, he'd never see her be one of those women. She loved her food. A lot. And had a healthy appetite and was lucky that it didn't pack pounds on her. She set down her empty cup. "I'm ready to go." Enough of this talk about her eating.

When they got outside, she tilted her face to the sun, feeling the warm rays wash over her. It was going to be a scorcher today. Hardly any wind, and bright sunny skies. Seemed strange to think a big storm was headed their way with clear skies like this.

They headed down the sidewalk toward the community center, side by side. His arm brushed hers every once and again but she ignored it. Really.

They passed by Cone Corner and she reminded herself it was ridiculous to be craving an ice cream cone after the big breakfast she'd just consumed. But maybe she'd grab one later...

Noah greeted them as they walked into the center. "Ah, workers." Noah gave her a quick hug.

"Where can we help?" Mason asked.

"Mind getting the rest of the shutters up?"

"Sure thing," Mason readily agreed.

"I'm going to set up some tables. Some of the ladies from town are already bringing food here. Cookies. Cakes. And the fridge is starting to fill up, too. We'll at least be eating good while we wait out the storm." Noah headed off to the storeroom to grab the tables.

Never let it be said that the townsfolk of Belle Island would ever let anyone go hungry.

CHAPTER 5

Lillian wandered back to The Nest after dealing with a late evening guest issue. Gary was out walking Lucky—which was where she'd planned on being, too, before she was called away. She slipped inside and peace settled around her. The Nest. Her sanctuary, her refuge, her haven. Inside these walls, she could almost—*almost*—believe all the problems in the world didn't exist. Not even the storm.

She sat down in her recliner and picked up the leather journal sitting on the table beside her. Gary had found it hidden in Magnolia House when he was doing some rehab on the house, and she hadn't had much luck finding the family of the young woman, Anna, who'd written it. She'd love to return this piece of history to them. If only she could actually locate who the family was.

She read a few more entries but found out nothing to help her with her search for Anna's family. She turned one more page and exclaimed as she read the words. Johnny's father was the lightkeeper at the lighthouse. Now that was a clue that might help. Reading the journal had shown her one thing for certain, though. This Anna who wrote in the journal was in love with Johnny. And Anna's father did not approve of Johnny. Not one bit.

She let out a long sigh, admitting she was a hopeless romantic. She just hoped Anna had ended up with her Johnny. But would she ever find out if Anna did?

She set down the journal and picked up her knitting, hoping to settle her nervous energy as well as her racing mind before Gary came back. Her mind galloped along as she worked on her knitting in spite of every effort to quit thinking about the upcoming storm or the mysterious Anna and Johnny.

Gary walked in from the deck. "Ah, you're here." He smiled at her and let Lucky off the leash.

"Did you have a nice walk?"

"We did. Missed you, though." He walked over and pressed a kiss to the top of her head.

"The guest problem was really a non-problem, but I do like to keep them all happy. There are hardly any guests left now that they've said the storm has intensified. No evacuation orders, though."

"Maybe it will fizzle out at sea."

"We can only hope." She looked down at her knitting and realized she'd dropped a stitch. Maybe now wasn't the best time to knit.

"Want something to drink?" Gary headed toward the kitchen.

"No, I'm fine."

He returned with a glass of ice water and sat on the couch across from her. He nodded at the leather journal beside her chair. "Have you been reading more of it?"

"Just a bit. I did get one more clue. It's clear that Anna loved this Johnny she wrote about. And she said that Johnny's father is the lightkeeper."

"Really? That's interesting."

"I wonder if there's a list of lightkeepers at the historical society. Maybe a history of the lighthouse. If I can find out more about Johnny, maybe I can find out more about Anna." She gave him a sheepish smile. "And I hope to find out they ended up together.

"Ah, my sweet, sentimental wife." His eyes glowed with tenderness. "Just one of the many things I love about you.

Lillian set down her knitting. "Well, there's not really time to search now. Maybe after the storm." She stood up. "You ready for bed?"

"I am. It's been a long day."

"And another long one tomorrow while we wait and watch the storm."

Gary stood, took her hand, and they headed off to bed. She was very grateful to have him by her side this week while they prepared for the storm.

LATE THAT EVENING Robin and Jay walked home from the inn. She wanted to walk hand-in-hand with him, but she was sure someone would see them. Then within minutes, everyone in town would know about them.

She really needed to find time to talk to Sara and Charlotte first. They'd be mad at her if they found out from town gossip. She'd tell them both tomorrow. With that decision made, she felt better. Tomorrow she'd walk home with Jay's arm around her and wouldn't care who saw them.

"I need to let Barney out. Mind if we stop by my house first?" Jay asked, oblivious to her decision and the fact they'd be walking home arm in arm tomorrow.

She smiled to herself, still lost in her thoughts of letting the world know that she and Jay were a couple. Bringing herself back to reality, she looked up at Jay. "How's Barney adjusting to living with you?"

"He's doing fine."

"Bet he misses Mrs. Gleason. He was used to someone being home almost all day."

"I'm glad I could take him in when she couldn't have Barney at her retirement place. I actually like having him around." Jay opened the door to his house.

Barney walked past them out into the yard. They stood on the porch, but she was dying to peek inside and see what havoc Barney had wreaked on Jay's house while he'd been gone. When she'd kept Barney a few weeks ago for

Mrs. Gleason, he had destroyed anything and everything he could reach. Jay was going to find out soon enough that Barney equaled disaster.

Barney trotted back up the steps and they followed him inside. She looked around in amazement. No pillows from the couch on the floor. No chewed up shoes or books. She turned to Jay. "How come he's not destroying everything at your house?"

Jay grinned. "We had a talk. I told him not to."

"Ah, a dog whisperer. Who knew?"

"I've got beer in the fridge. Want one? We could sit out on the deck for a bit, then I'll walk you home."

"Sounds good." They grabbed beers and settled on a loveseat on the deck overlooking the bay. Jay had a great view and she was a bit jealous. Her porch looked out on some common ground at the group of bungalows. They had access to the bay down a walkway, but no view from her bungalow.

She kicked off her shoes and curled her legs under her, taking a sip of the ice-cold beer. "Ah, that's good."

Jay's lips curved into a smile that sent her pulse racing. "It is good."

"You haven't tasted yours yet." She cocked her head.

"Maybe I wasn't talking about the beer. Maybe I was talking about being here with you." He leaned down and kissed her slowly, leisurely, as if he were enjoying every single slow-moving moment.

She let out a sigh as he pulled away. "Ah, that was good, too."

He laughed. "It was."

He draped his arm around her shoulder and they sat in the moonlight, silent. And everything was right with her world.

Until she looked around for Barney. "Hey, where did Barney go?"

Jay glanced around. "I left the slider open. He must have gone inside."

"Oh, no..." She looked down at where she'd slipped off her shoes. One lone shoe rested there. "Barney..." She jumped up and rushed inside.

Barney rested on the couch, looking innocent. But her other shoe sat on the floor, a chewed up, ruined mess.

"Barney!" She leaned down and snatched her shoe, waving it toward Jay. "See, that dog has it out for me."

"Barney, we talked about that. No chewing on anything but your toys," Jay spoke sternly to the dog.

Robin swore the dog rolled his eyes at Jay...

CHAPTER 6

The next day Betty Gleason looked around the lunchroom of the retirement center. She'd been eating in her apartment since she moved in, but it was time to wander out and meet people. She suddenly felt like a young girl in high school, waiting to be invited to sit with someone. She stood still, holding her tray of food, looking for a place to sit, a group that looked friendly to join.

"Betty Gleason, is that you? I didn't know you were moving here."

She looked into the friendly face of Ida, an acquaintance from Belle Island. "Ida, so good to see someone I know."

"Come, sit with George and me. We're just over there by the window."

Betty followed Ida over to the table and took an empty seat, grateful to feel less like an outsider.

"Betty, good to see you. Did you just move in?" George smiled.

"I did. Still trying to get settled. It's... it's quite an adjustment. But my daughter... well, she wanted me to move here. And I'm closer to her, so it will make things easier on her. I—I had a little car accident and I wasn't driving anymore. It was hard on my daughter to come over from the mainland to the island to bring me to appointments and things. But I've lived on the island my whole life. My momma grew up there, too. We've been there for generations, but I was the last one." She let out a long sigh. "It's very hard to live anywhere but Belle Island."

"We're closer to our kids and grandkids now, too." George nodded. "And, I admit, it was getting hard to keep up with Magnolia House. It was just so... big. Way too big for just the two of us."

"I did love that house, though." Ida sighed.

"I had moved to those cute little bungalows on the bay. Do you know them?"

"Oh, I do. I think Robin and Charlotte live there, too. Don't they?"

"They do. They lived right next door. They were such sweet neighbors." Betty reached for some cream to put in her coffee. Her daughter insisted it wasn't good for her, but she loved cream in her coffee and she might as well indulge a bit. "And you know Jay, the chef from Charming Inn?"

"We do. A fine young man," George said.

"I couldn't bring my dog Barney, and I couldn't find him a home. I was going to have to give him to the beagle rescue group. It was breaking my heart. I was so worried about where he'd end up. But Jay offered to take Barney. I was so relieved."

"I bet you miss him though." Ida's voice was filled with sympathy.

"So much. It was the main reason I kept resisting coming here. But Jay said he'd bring Barney to visit. I can't wait. And look, he's already sent a picture of Barney." Betty took out her phone and showed them a photo of Barney sitting on Jay's deck.

"I'm sorry you couldn't have him here, but at least you found him a good home and you'll still get to see him." Ida sent her a sympathetic smile. "Life sends us unexpected changes as we get older. We have to learn to deal with them."

"We do." She bobbed her head. "But I'm very thankful to Jay."

"So, we went back to the island a bit ago and spoke to Lillian. You know she bought Magnolia House, right?" Ida asked.

"I heard that."

"Anyway, she had this man—Gary—working on fixing the place up."

"Lillian married Gary," Betty interrupted.

"We heard that, too." Ida nodded. "We try to keep up with all the news from the island. Anyway, Gary found this old journal hidden behind a board at Magnolia House. Isn't that interesting? Lillian is trying to figure out who the family is of the woman who wrote it."

"Oh, like some kind of mystery."

"I've been wondering if she's found out any more about the family of the girl who wrote it."

"I don't know, but I'll be sure and ask when Jay brings Barney to visit. Maybe he'll know. He's bringing Barney to visit me after the storm." Betty tried a bite of her meal. Surprisingly tasty, much better than she thought the meals would be in the dining room here at the retirement center.

"I do hope the storm weakens and Belle Island fairs well through it." Ida's forehead wrinkled with concern.

"I do, too. And I worry about Barney. He's not a big fan of storms."

"I'm sure Jay will take good care of him," George said.

"Oh, I'm sure he will." But she still worried about her Barney. She sighed and took a sip of her coffee with the cream. Very good. Even if her daughter would be disappointed in her choice. Her daughter was one of those people who picked a new diet fad every six months or so. Her daughter's new one included no dairy. No coffee either, for that matter. That was never going to happen for her. She planned on enjoying her coffee until her last days.

She turned from her thoughts back to the conversation with George and Ida. She enjoyed the easy conversation with them. Maybe this move wouldn't be so bad if she could get to know more people here. Though she'd still rather be back on her beloved Belle Island.

CHAPTER 7

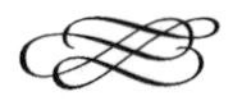

Robin hurried through the inn the next morning. She'd just checked the last guests out. Well, all the guests except for Zoe and Mason. They were staying, but they were more family than guests. Mason insisted on staying to be near his father and Lillian in case they needed help. And Zoe? She was pretty sure Zoe wanted to stay because Mason was staying. She'd seen the looks they'd been giving each other.

And Lillian and Gary would be at The Nest, of course, to watch over things.

The storm predictions weren't good, and the authorities had recommended all non-residents leave the island. Luckily the handful of remaining guests had agreed and gone home. She didn't envy them the long drive up the highway in the heavy traffic with everyone trying to escape the storm.

She and Jay would stay, though. Help Lillian. If it got too bad, they'd all head to the community center. They'd done it before. It was just life on this small Florida island.

The storm was predicted to hit tomorrow as a category one hurricane. Still hitting north of here, but the winds would be vicious on the island and there could be localized flooding.

She got to the kitchen and Jay looked up from where he was cleaning the counters and smiled at her. He tilted his head toward the supply cabinet with a small nod and a wink. She grinned and followed him inside.

He took her into his arms and kissed her. "Ah, now that's more like it. Been wanting to do that since I said good night to you last night."

"You should try it again, just in case it's a while until you can do it again," she teased.

"Good plan, woman." He kissed her again, pulling her close.

The door swung open to the storage room

and she looked over in surprise. Sara stood in the doorway, an amused look on her face.

"So this is where you two hide out." Sara shook her head, a wide smile on her face. "About time you two got together."

"Sara, I was going to tell you and Charlotte. I was going to tell you *today*. Honest." Robin disentangled herself from Jay's arms and went over to her friend.

"How long has this been going on?"

"Just a few days. Since Sunday. It's just been so crazy with everyone getting ready for the storm..."

Sara gave her a quick hug. "I'm happy for you. And it's about time. I just came to tell you I'm headed to the community center to help Noah." She turned to leave. "But you better tell Charlotte about you two before the news gets out."

"I'll go find her now," Robin promised.

Jay walked over to her. "So, if you tell Charlotte, does that mean we don't have to hide out in the storage room to kiss?"

She smiled up at him. "That's exactly what it means. You can kiss me any time you want."

"And I'll want to kiss you lots. A whole lot. Frequently." An infectious grin spread across his face. "So, go find her. I'm going to close up the kitchen and see what Lillian needs me to do. I'll catch up with you later."

They walked out of the storage closet and Dana pretended not to notice.

"Hey, Dana. Why don't you head out? I'll finish up here." Jay headed over to the counter where he'd been working before their little storage closet escapade.

"Are you sure?"

"I'm sure."

Dana took off her apron, a worried look on her face. "I... could help."

"No, I'm good. Go home and stay safe."

Dana nodded and left through the kitchen's back door.

Robin walked over and gave Jay another quick kiss. "Okay, I'm outta here. I'll go find Charlotte."

Robin hurried off and found Charlotte at the bungalow. "There you are."

Charlotte turned to her. "I'm wrapping some of my paintings and putting them over at the loft above the marina. It's higher there. Just in case there is flooding."

"That's a good plan. Let me help."

Charlotte handed her a roll of plastic. They

wrapped the paintings and she helped Charlotte load them in her car. Charlotte turned to go, and Robin reached out and grabbed her arm. "Before you leave..."

Charlotte turned back to her.

"I... I need to talk to you about something. I mean... just wanted to tell you."

"Spill it." Charlotte looked at her questioningly.

"It's about Jay. About me and Jay."

Charlotte laughed. "I already know. I figured you'd tell me when you were ready. Anyway, I heard you guys out on the porch last night and glanced out the window. That was some kiss." She grinned.

"I thought you were asleep when I got home."

"I headed to bed after I spied you two. In case you came inside for some privacy." Charlotte shook her head. "But you better tell Sara."

"She knows." Robin grinned. "She caught us kissing in the supply cabinet at the inn."

Charlotte's laughter rang out across the courtyard. "So much for your secret."

"I didn't mean to keep it a secret. Not from you two."

"And now you haven't. I couldn't be happier for you and Jay. It was obvious you two were meant to be together. I was hoping you'd work things out." Charlotte hugged her. "Now I've got to run. I'll catch up with you later."

"See you later." Robin watched as Charlotte drove away. Now the whole world could know she and Jay were a couple.

And she couldn't be more pleased.

ROBIN WENT BACK to the inn and pulled out her to-do list. Almost everything regarding the storm was checked off. She picked up a package that had been delivered for Lillian and went to find her.

Lillian was in the dining room talking to Jay. He gave her a quick smile. "I was just telling Lillian that... um... well, that you and I... worked things out."

She walked up to him with what was probably a silly grin on her face and took his hand. "Yes, we did."

"About time." Lillian shook her head. "Took you two forever to see what I could see plain as day. For years. What *everyone* could see. Now you two just be sure you make it work."

"Oh, it will work. I won't let her get away again." He squeezed her hand.

Robin smiled up at Jay, then turned back to Lillian. "This package came for you. It's from Etta at the historical society. She must have dropped it off earlier."

"She said she'd send over some research she did. She's helping me with trying to figure out if Anna and Johnny in the journal ever got together." Lillian gave a little laugh. "I so hope they did."

Lillian took the package and opened it, glancing inside. "Oh, a note from Etta."

Robin watched while a look of sadness swept over Lillian's face. "What's wrong?"

Lillian cleared her throat. "Etta said that she found an article about casualties of a hurricane that went through here back in the late eighteen hundreds. Anna talked about an approaching storm in her journal. Anna Smith was listed as one of the townsfolk who was missing and presumed dead."

"Oh, no."

Lillian blinked and cleared her throat. "I know it's silly. I don't even know her personally.

It's just that I feel like I *did* know her from reading her journal. I had skipped ahead in the journal a while ago, and she'd mentioned a storm was coming. Then I decided to just read everything in order and went back to the beginning. Now I want to hurry and finish up. I guess it will end with the storm..."

"I'm sorry, Lillian."

Lillian sighed. "I had just hoped that Anna and her Johnny-beau had ended up together." Lillian slipped the note back in the package. "Well, I should go find Gary. And I'll go put this in The Nest. Time to concentrate on our own storm."

"What can I do to help now?" Jay asked.

"Did you send Dana home?"

"I did."

"Would you mind checking and seeing if Magnolia House is all battened down?"

"Yes, of course." Jay nodded.

"I'll go with him unless you need me here?"

"No, that's about it. And thank you. You two have been working tirelessly getting things prepared. But I think that's about it for today. You two have a safe place to stay during the storm?"

"She's going to stay with me," Jay said and turned to her.

Surprise swept through her. He hadn't said anything to her or asked her. But she had to admit, she'd feel better staying with him than staying alone in the bungalow.

"Don't argue. I'll feel better if you do. Charlotte can come, too." His eyes implored her.

"She's staying at Ruby's with Ben."

"If it gets bad, you two go to the community center," Lillian admonished them.

"We will," Jay assured her.

Lillian hurried off and Robin turned to Jay. "So, I'm staying with you, huh? What will the town think?"

"The town can think what they want. I just want to keep you safe."

"Maybe I'm saying yes that I'll stay with you because I want to keep *you* safe." A smile tugged at her lips.

"That works, too." He winked then took her hand and they headed over to check on Magnolia House.

Jay was glad Robin hadn't argued about staying with him to ride out the storm. There was no way he was comfortable with her staying alone in her bungalow. They'd just hunker down at his house and wait until it passed by them. Didn't sound like a bad way to spend time...

He walked around the outside of Magnolia House while Robin checked on things inside. All they had left was to pull the hurricane protection over the back door as they left.

Jay went inside. "The wind is picking up a bit."

"So it begins." Robin paused and frowned. "Do you hear that?"

"Hear what? I just hear the wind."

"No, it's like a crying sound." She walked around the room a few steps, her forehead creased in concentration. "There it is again."

"Probably just the wind in the trees or it's making the wires sing a bit."

"No... that's not it." She walked out on the back steps and climbed down the stairs.

He followed her out, still not hearing anything.

She stood outside, then suddenly, bending down low, she peeked under the steps. "Ah, ha!" She reached under and came out with a tiny kitten in her hands. "Hello little guy. What are you doing out all alone? Don't you know a storm is coming?" She petted the frightened kitten and talked soothingly to it until it started to purr.

Jay climbed down the stairs and stood beside her. "Kitten, this is your lucky day. You don't want to be out here right now."

"Doesn't look to be more than six or eight weeks old, does it?" She glanced up at him.

He shrugged. "I'm not the expert on kittens. I just got my first dog, remember?"

"I'm taking him home with us. He can't stay out here."

"Not sure how that will go over with Barney..." Jay shook his head, not that he'd ever refuse Robin anything. "But you're right, we can't just leave the little guy out in the storm to fend for himself."

Jay closed the door, pulled the hurricane protection across it, and they headed back to his house. They passed by the inn and Jay frowned. "Is that Dana? What's she doing here?"

"I don't know."

"I'll go check." He jogged toward the side of the inn. "Dana," he called out as he got close.

She whirled around to face him. A look of what he could only describe as panic or fear crossed her face.

"You okay?"

"Uh... Yes."

She didn't look okay.

"I thought you left and went home."

"I did... I just... forgot something. I'm, um, leaving now." Dana looked back at the door to the kitchen.

"You sure you're okay?"

Dana looked right at him. "It's just— I—" She stopped abruptly and shrugged. "Storm just has me jumpy, I guess."

"I'll lock up again." He nodded to her. "You go home. Wind is picking up."

Dana nodded slowly, then turned and walked away. He didn't see her carrying anything. *Wonder what she forgot?* He shook his head and locked the door—one of the few hurricane doors on the inn so it needed no extra protection—and trotted back to where Robin and the kitten waited for him.

"Everything okay?"

"Yeah, she just forgot something. All locked up again."

They hurried along the streets and ran into

Mrs. Peabody closing the pet shop. "Hey, Mrs. Peabody. Could we grab a bag of kitten food?" Jay asked. "Robin found this little guy hiding under the stairs."

Mrs. Peabody reached out and petted the kitten. "Glad you found her before the storm. I've got the register all shut down, but I'll grab you a bag."

"It's a her?" Robin asked.

"Let me look." Mrs. Peabody gently picked up the kitten and looked at it. "Yes, you have a female."

"Thank you, so much." Robin took the kitten back. "Now I can name her properly.

Jay eyed her. So, it was looking like the kitten was getting to be more a permanent resident with Robin. He wasn't surprised. She had the kindest heart of anyone he knew. Wonder how Barney was going to handle this new addition?

Mrs. Peabody returned with a small bag of kitten food. "Here, you'll want to moisten it."

"Thanks, appreciate this." Jay took the bag as Mrs. Peabody locked up the door again.

"Stay safe," Mrs. Peabody said.

"You, too." Robin said as they turned away and headed down the sidewalk.

Jay wrapped his arm protectively around

Robin while she cradled the kitten snuggled up against her.

This? Just this walking down the sidewalk with Robin next to him? It felt... well, it just felt *right.*

CHAPTER 8

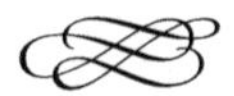

Zoe had to admit every muscle in her body ached from the work they'd done the last few days at the community center. Lugging things around. Putting up the hurricane protection. On her feet almost all day long. She was a regular at her gym back home, but this work had exhausted her. Maybe it was the work plus stress of worrying about the approaching storm. She'd never quite gotten used to the stress of the waiting.

She knew Noah was torn between glad she was here and wishing she'd headed back inland. And he hadn't been pleased to hear she was staying at the inn instead of coming to stay at his house with him and Sara. But she was glad she'd convinced him that Lillian might need her help.

She sat on the edge of her bed at the inn, trying to get up the energy to get dressed after her shower. The shower she'd hoped would not only wash off the grime of the day but revitalize her.

So far, no dice.

She and Mason had been invited for a light dinner at The Nest with Lillian and Gary. She *really* needed to get dressed. Like right now. Mason would be here in minutes. She pushed off the bed and shrugged on a pair of shorts, a t-shirt, and flip-flops. Good enough.

She answered the door at the first knock. Mason stood there looking refreshed, snappily dressed in khaki shorts and a knitted collared shirt, and not a bit tired.

"You ready?" Mason stepped inside her room.

She looked down at her old shorts and faded Lighthouse Point t-shirt. Then she glanced around, wishing she'd picked things up. The clothes she'd been wearing earlier today were in a pile near the bathroom. Clothes spilled out of her suitcase. Three pairs of shoes created a line from the suitcase to the closet. The closet where she'd only hung up a few things and the closet door stood wide open.

"Uh, yes, let's go." They should leave and close the door on this mess. She'd clean it all up when she got back to the room tonight. Maybe he hadn't really noticed, but she doubted that. Mason was... neat. And dressed much nicer than she was. Well, nothing she could do about that now. She couldn't actually ask him to stand out in the hall while she planned her wardrobe a bit better, now could she?

"I'm famished. Glad Lil invited us." Mason walked back out without saying a word about the chaos that was her room or her very, very casual attire.

She tugged the door behind them and followed him along the long hallway and down the stairs. They cut across the inn towards The Nest. The inn was eerily spooky with no guests roaming around. The wind had picked up and rattled the shutters over the windows.

"Kind of creepy," she admitted to Mason as she moved a bit closer to him.

"Looks like one of those scenes in a horror film. The darkened empty inn. The howling wind. This is where, in the movie, a woman would walk out into a garage or shed, or up to the attic by herself, to see what the noise was that she heard." He grinned at her.

She laughed. "It does look exactly like a scene from a movie like that. But it is creepy like this."

"Come on." He took her hand in his and led her toward The Nest.

His strong hand wrapped around hers did make her feel better. She took one last glance back at the deserted lobby area.

They got to The Nest and Gary let them in. "Welcome. I'm not sure what Lillian is making for what she calls a *light* dinner, but it smells wonderful. Lillian, Mason and Zoe are here."

Lillian poked her head out from the kitchen. "It's just soup and salad. Nothing fancy. And I stole some rolls and a pie from the inn's kitchen. Gary, why don't you make them drinks while I finish up?"

"Beer, wine, soda?"

"Beer for me," Mason said as they walked into the room.

"Red wine?" Zoe asked.

"Have a nice merlot opened. I'll get some of that."

Gary returned with their drinks and they all stood inside the sliding door to the deck overlooking the beach. The palm fronds danced wildly in the wind, slashing against each other.

"This door has hurricane impact windows in it so it doesn't need shutters over it. Lillian said when she had to replace the door a year or so ago, she replaced it with this one. At least we can still look out and see what's going on." Gary stood nursing his drink.

She looked out at the waves that were starting to hammer the beach as the winds picked up. The pure power of these storms frightened her and fascinated her at the same time.

"Come on to the kitchen," Lillian called. "Dinner's ready."

She followed Gary and Mason into the kitchen. Lillian had set the table with cheerful placemats and plain white dishes. She noticed that Lillian had placed candles and matches nearby. That made sense in case the electricity went out. One thing she'd learned when she'd first moved to the island with Noah. Always have candles and flashlights ready. Electricity was iffy during any storm here.

Gary and Mason talked business while they ate. She chatted with Lillian about a few changes that Sara was making to Noah's house to make it feel less like a bachelor pad. It felt like a normal family dinner. She'd missed her family dinners with Noah since she'd moved away. For a bit, she even managed to forget about the storm.

For a bit. Kind of.

They all sat and ate their dinner and finished it off with peach pie. Not really her definition of light, but she'd amazed herself at how hungry she was. And she was finally beginning to perk up after the meal.

Over Lillian's protests, Zoe and Mason sent her and Gary to the living room and did the dishes. Afterward, Zoe looked around at the cleaned-up kitchen.

"We should probably go," she whispered to Mason. "Lillian and Gary were supposed to be on their honeymoon right now. Not preparing for a storm, or feeding us."

"Yes, their marriage has certainly started out with a bit of chaos. You're right, we should go."

They headed out to where Gary and Lillian were sitting. Lillian had her knitting in her lap, but her knitting needles lay quiet.

"Dad, we're going to go now."

"You sure? You could stay for a while."

"I'm really tired," Zoe quickly added, wanting to give them their privacy. "But thank you so much for the dinner."

Gary rose and walked them to the door. "Good night. We'll talk to you in the morning. Come down for breakfast and we'll know better about the storm by then."

"Sounds good. We will." Mason nodded.

"Good night," Lillian called from her recliner, her knitting needles finally moving in rhythm.

"Night," Zoe answered as she and Mason slipped out the door.

"So are you really tired?" Mason paused after a few steps. "Want to come to my room for some wine?" Mason gave her one of his impish, impossible to resist smiles.

"I was tired... but I seem to have found my second wind. Another glass of wine sounds like just the thing."

When they got to Mason's room, he switched on a lamp on the desk. The low light made the room feel intimate and inviting as she followed him inside. He crossed over to the dresser and picked up two bottles of wine, one in each hand. "Merlot or cab?"

"Either." Zoe shrugged.

"I snagged two glasses from the dining room, earlier. Always pays to be prepared." He poured them both a glass of merlot and handed her one. "To weathering the storm."

"To weathering the storm." She raised her glass to his, hoping the island did fare well through all this.

Mason walked over and pulled out the desk chair for her. "Here, have a seat."

She sat down, and he paced the room slowly. The light from the one lamp cast a cozy light around them, but it still felt strange with the windows boarded up and no glimpse at the outside world.

"It's dark in here with the shutters up." He turned back toward her. "Wish we could see out like we could at Lillian's."

Okay then, they were thinking the same thoughts now. How could they be so in sync when they'd only known each other a week or so?

"I know. That's one of the things I hate about these storms. You just sit and wait and wonder."

He finally settled down on the edge of the bed. "I've never been through anything like this before. Lillian gave me a battery-powered lantern and another flashlight. They're over on the dresser if we need them."

She took a sip of the wine as silence fell between them. Mason shifted on the bed. She sat stiffly on the chair.

"Listen... um... why don't you come over here? You look uncomfortable. We'll pile the pillows up on the bed and just relax there?" Mason suggested.

She looked from him to the decidedly comfortable bed with its stack of pillows and rose. "Sounds a lot more comfortable."

He kicked off his shoes and scooted up to the head of the bed. She slipped off her flip-flops, handed him her wine, and climbed up from the foot of the bed. She settled next to him, leaning back on the pillows. He handed her back her glass of wine and she took another sip, ignoring how close he was to her. Inches away. Ignoring the rush of her pulse. Ignoring the heat of his body so close to her. Yes, she ignored all of that.

She glanced over at him, but he seemed unaffected by how close they were sitting, her racing pulse, or her riotous thoughts. So maybe their thoughts weren't in sync now...

"Strange couple of days it's been." Mason

adjusted a pillow behind him and leaned back again, still looking incredibly relaxed.

She was wound tighter than an eight-day clock. She frowned. Where had she heard that saying before? It wasn't one that normally came to mind. She shook her head at her crazy thoughts and answered him. "It has been strange. Lillian and Gary's wedding, then all the work to get ready for the storm."

He smiled at her in the dim light of the lamp. "But, I've really enjoyed being able to spend time with you."

As she searched his face, a look of tenderness mixed with desire filtered through his golden-brown eyes. He reached over and took her wine glass again and set it on the nightstand.

She swallowed, her racing pulse now galloping through her veins and her heart beating in a syncopated rhythm.

"And another thing." He turned back to her, his gaze no longer leaving her face. "I'd sure like to kiss you again. I've been wanting to since that goodbye kiss on Sunday. Think that would be okay?"

She nodded silently. Yes, that would be okay. Better than okay. Then she closed her eyes as his warm lips settled on hers, his strong hand encircling the back of her neck as he pulled her closer.

When he finally let her go, her breath came out in quick gasps. Oh, the man knew how to kiss...

He tilted her chin up and looked into her eyes, searching her face. Then he brushed a thumb across her jawline. "You're a very interesting woman, Zoe Birch. Can't think of anyone I'd rather ride out the storm with."

Her heart pounded furiously in her chest, matching the fury of the wind outside, as he leaned down and kissed her again. And then again.

As far as she was concerned, he could kiss her all through the stormy night.

CHAPTER 9

Robin followed Jay into his house. Barney looked up at them with a bored expression until he spied the kitten tucked in her arms. He got up, stretched, walked over, and stared up at her. She swore his face held an accusing look.

"Barney, you need to leave the kitten alone," Jay warned the dog, then nodded at her. "Go ahead, put the kitten down."

She gently set the kitten down, ready to scoop it up at the first sign of the dog being too rough. Barney sniffed the animal a few times, turned, and walked away.

"Well, I guess that's it." She admitted she was surprised. She'd thought that Barney would pester the kitty or... something.

"Told you Barney listens to me." Jay headed to the kitchen. "I'll get you a bowl to feed the kitten and I'll get some dinner started for us."

She fed the kitten and then leaned against a counter watching Jay make up some delicious smelling stir fry dish from items he'd found in his fridge. It sure paid to date a chef, that much was for certain.

"Oh, did you get the camera installed in Lillian's office?"

"I did. I need to set up alerts and make sure Lillian knows how to shut it off when she's in her office if she doesn't want it on."

"I can't believe more money is missing. That's so crazy. Why is someone targeting the inn? It's not like we have huge cash deposits or anything. And since the first theft, we've been making an effort to take the deposit in every day."

"I don't know, but I'd sure like to catch whoever is doing it. Not only because I caught the blame for the first theft, but because I can't believe someone would steal from Lillian. She's so kindhearted and giving."

Robin frowned. "I do hope we figure it out. I know it's really bothering Lillian."

"Of course it is. Not only is the money missing, but someone is invading her space, her privacy."

Jay served up the food and they sat at the table. The kitten wandered around under their feet while Barney sat in the corner, watching. The kitten brushed up against her leg and she reached down to pet it. The kitty finally roamed over to Barney and sat there for a moment, then reached out to paw at Barney.

Barney wasn't having it. He swatted at the kitten and made a noise. Not quite a growl, but a definite back off sound.

"Barney, be nice. The kitten is just a tiny thing," Jay admonished the dog.

The kitten came back over to the table and she scooped her up. "I think I should name her."

"You planning on keeping her?" Jay eyed her.

"Probably?" She wouldn't mind having company at her bungalow. Charlotte would be moving out after she married Ben. The bungalow would just feel... empty. Maybe she could become a crazy cat lady and talk to her cat all the time.

"You're keeping her. I can tell." Jay shook

his head, but a small smile played at the corners of his mouth. "You should probably have a name for her then."

She paused and looked at the kitten in her arms. She was a small, orange and white tabby, with bright, curious eyes. I think I'll call her Sunny. She looks like a Sunny, doesn't she?"

"I guess so?" Doubt hovered in Jay's eyes. "Seems strange to name a cat Sunny in the middle of a storm..."

"I think it fits her perfectly."

Jay rose. "I'm going to clear the dishes and we can go in and sit in the front room. I want to pull up the weather, too. See if there are any changes."

"I'll help." She stood, set Sunny on the floor, and grabbed her dishes. They stood side by side at the sink, rinsing the dishes and putting them in the dishwasher. Good to know Jay was a rinse off well before loading dishwasher person like she was. Charlotte barely ran a trace of water on the dishes before dropping them into the dishwasher. She'd been known to go behind Charlotte and re-rinse the dishes.

They finished up the dishes and settled onto the couch in the front room. Sunny immediately jumped up and started walking all over them.

Jay raised his eyebrows in surprise before his expression turned to one of amused affection. Barney sat near their feet but eyed the roving kitten.

A sudden gust of wind rattled the shutters. Jay grabbed his phone and checked the forecast. "Still at the same level but there's one predictor who thinks the storm might shift to the south."

"That's not good." Robin sighed. "Storms are so stressful. The waiting. The wondering when and where they'll hit."

"We'll be fine."

She appreciated his words of assurance, but of course, no one knew if they would be fine. If the storm intensified and the island took a direct hit...

She felt his fingers on her chin, turning her face to look at him. "We'll be fine, Robs."

"I hope so." She settled against him and let Sunny's antics entertain them. At least for now, she could pretend all that was happening outside didn't exist. They were safe, cocooned up in Jay's house.

CHAPTER 10

A dull throbbing of his arm roused Mason, and then a sensation of pins and needles shot up his arm. Opening his eyes slowly, he looked down to see Zoe in his arms, curled up next to him, sound asleep.

The last thing he remembered was them sitting on his bed, talking, asking questions, getting to know each other better. And the kisses. There had definitely been quite a lot of kissing going on.

He smiled down at her and carefully shifted a wayward lock of hair from her face. Her breathing came in slow, even breaths. Her lashes rested near her rosy cheeks. She looked so incredibly peaceful. He hated to move his arm, to disturb her.

The one lone lamp cast a protective low glow around them. He shifted slightly wondering if he could pull his arm free without disturbing her. But then, he didn't really want to move her out of his arms.

A steady glaring alarm interrupted the peace. He looked down and saw Zoe stirring, then her eyes popped open. Then opened wider and she shot up and scooted a bit away from him. Her forehead wrinkled. "What's the noise?"

"I'm not sure."

She snatched her phone from her pocket and looked at it. "It's an alert. The storm is gathering strength and now it's aimed right at us. We're supposed to evacuate."

"What... well, what do we do in that instance?" He knew nothing about hurricanes except what he'd occasionally see on the news. And they never seemed quite real to him, always far, far away.

This one sure seemed real enough.

A banging at the door drew his attention and he heard his father's voice. "Mason, wake up. We need to get off the island."

He pushed off the bed, swinging and shaking his arm to chase away the numbness, and hurried over to open the door. His father looked past him at Zoe sitting on the bed but said nothing about finding her here in his room. In his bed...

"Let's go. We need to evacuate. Meet us downstairs in five minutes. We're leaving. You two should ride with us."

Zoe was climbing off the bed and answering her phone that was now ringing. "Noah, yes, we heard. We're heading out." She paused and looked over at Gary. "No, you don't have to come get me. Gary said we could ride with them. We'll meet up with you later on the mainland."

She clicked off her phone and turned to him. "Noah is making sure the people at the community center have rides off the island, then he and Sara are headed to the mainland."

"Five minutes," his father said again and disappeared.

"I need to grab a few things from my room. Two minutes. I swear." Zoe rushed past him and over to her room next to his.

He glanced around the room, grabbed his laptop, and shoved it into its case, along with some paperwork. He threw his toiletries into a carryon and added a change of clothes. Good enough.

He met Zoe in the hallway. She was carrying a duffle with her things. They hurried down to The Nest. The wind had picked up even more, and they struggled against it as they hurried out to Gary's SUV, tossing their few things inside as they climbed in. Lucky climbed onto Lillian's lap as Gary started the motor. They headed toward Main Street and then turned toward the road to the bridge. There they were met with a line of cars. None of them moving.

"Is this normal?" Mason peered out at the traffic.

"No. It should be moving. Slowly, but moving." Lillian frowned.

He saw a man walking down the line of cars, pausing at each one. He got to their car and his father rolled down the window.

Lillian leaned over to peer out the window. "Sheriff Dave, what's happening here?"

"A large tug and another boat pulled loose and hit the bridge. We're not sure it's safe to cross. Looks like some major damage. We're asking people to head back to the community center. I'm trying to get the city alert system to send out the alert about it."

Just then Lillian and Zoe's phones rang with the alert sound. Lillian glanced at hers. "Here it is. Hopefully, people will get the message."

"We'll head there now." Gary rolled up the window.

Slowly, one by one, the cars got enough room between them to turn around. Gary swung around in his turn and headed to the community center. He pulled up as close to the center as he could get. "You all get out here. I'll go park. Mason, watch over Lillian and Lucky."

He nodded to his father as he helped Lillian out of the vehicle.

"I'm fine. Don't worry about me." Lillian kept a firm grip on Lucky's leash and darted toward the door to the community center.

Zoe appeared at his side and they rushed through the rain, following Lillian into the center.

Once inside, he blinked his eyes, adjusting to the light. Sara sat at a table by the door, taking down everyone's name as they entered. She jumped up and hugged Zoe. "Noah will be so glad to see you. He's been worried about you."

"The Yarnies will be getting food and hot coffee ready for everyone. I'm going to go help," Lillian said. "Will you tell Gary where I am when he gets inside?"

"Sure will." Sara wrote down Lillian's name on her list along with Zoe's and his.

"The Yarnies?" Mason asked.

"That's the knitting group here at the community center," Sara explained.

"Do you need help?" Mason offered, wanting to feel like he was doing something, anything. Maybe it would help take the edge off the uneasiness surging through him.

"Why don't you go find Noah? He'll know what needs to be done." Sara turned to a new group of people entering the center and wrote the names of a family of four.

Zoe took his hand and led him to the main room. The room was filled with people standing or sitting and talking in groups. A nervous energy crackled throughout the space but people remained calm.

Noah stood at the far end of the room, giving directions to people. He enveloped Zoe into a hug as soon as they got to him. "Ah, good. You're here. At least you're out of the storm. I should have sent you to safety days ago. I know how these storms can change." A deep look of concern etched Noah's features.

"Uncle Noah, I'll be fine. We all will. We'll just wait out the storm here at the center."

"What can we do to help?" Mason asked as he looked around at the crowd of people pouring into the room.

"There are more chairs in the storage area. Looks like we'll have a full house with the bridge closed. And bring in some blankets. Some of the people look soaked."

Good. Something to keep him busy. Zoe took his hand, again... he was getting kind of used to having her hand in his...

If he couldn't have her curled up in his arms, that is. He smiled to himself as she led him off to get the supplies and wondered if he could steal a quick kiss in the storage area.

CHAPTER 11

Robin couldn't sleep. The storm raged outside and her nerves matched its furor. She looked jealously at Jay sleeping peacefully on the couch. How he could sleep through the roar of the wind was a mystery. She got up and padded into the kitchen to make some tea. She flipped on one low under-counter light and opened the cabinets, searching silently.

"What are you looking for?" Jay came up behind her, his voice low and warm.

"I didn't mean to wake you."

"Had to get up to help you anyway." A smile played on his lips as he reached out and pulled her into his arms.

She snuggled up next to him, grateful for his strong arms around her. Glad she'd agreed to stay here with him. "I was looking for tea. I thought that might calm me down some."

"I have chamomile tea. Will that help?"

"You have chamomile?" That surprised her. He didn't seem a chamomile type of guy, if there was such a thing.

"My grandmother always loved to have a cup of it at night. It reminds me of her, so I keep some on hand." He let her go and put some water on to boil, then opened the cabinet next to the stove and took out the tea bags.

Who knew he was such a nostalgic person? Though she knew he missed his grandmother terribly. Even after being friends with him for five years, there were so many little things she didn't know about him.

They sat down at the table, waiting for the water to get hot.

"So, you can't sleep, huh?" He reached out and rubbed a thumb across the back of her hand.

The gesture was amazingly comforting. "I'm just restless. I rarely can sleep when we're on storm watch."

"Maybe the chamomile will help."

The subtle warm light surrounded them and for a few minutes, she didn't even mind the storm. It was peaceful just sitting here in the low light with Jay, waiting for their tea.

The peace was shattered with the jarring sound of an alert. She snatched her phone from her pocket as Jay did the same with his.

"Gotta get off the island, Robs." Jay rose in one swift motion and crossed over and turned off the stove. "Tea will have to wait until I can find you some after we're safely on the mainland and inland a ways."

She stood, knowing the drill. "I'll get my purse. And Sunny. We have to take Sunny and Barney."

He nodded. "Of course we will. You find Sunny and I'll get Barney's leash."

"I wish I had time to go home and grab some things in case we're trapped off the island for a few days."

"Sorry, Robs, no time. I'll grab a few things, though, and some food and water."

She went out to the front room and looked at where Sunny had been napping. No sign of her. "Sunny? Where are you? Kitty, kitty, kitty." She walked around calling for the kitten. Still no sign. She looked under the couch, behind the chairs, anywhere she could think of.

"Jay, I can't find Sunny. We can't just leave

her," she called out to him, a bit of panic racing through her. She didn't rescue the kitten only to have to leave her behind if she couldn't find her.

Jay strode into the room with the kitten in his arms. "Found her sound asleep on the pillow on my bed. Hope she doesn't think that's her new place to sleep. Because it's not..." Though the softness of his expression contradicted the sternness of his words.

She reached for Sunny and held her close. "Good kitty." She stroked Sunny's back and the kitten began to purr.

"I'll load up the car, then we'll leave."

Within a handful of minutes, Jay had the car loaded and they headed out. As they drove down the road, the rain began in earnest with the wipers barely clearing the windshield for them to peer out. Her heart pounded in her chest as they slowly drove with Jay straining to pay close attention to the road.

An alert from her phone grabbed her attention again. She slipped her phone out and read the alert. "Jay, the bridge. It's closed. It was damaged. The city alert said to go shelter at the community center."

He glanced over at her and nodded, a frown

creasing his face. "The bridge damaged? That's not good. Okay, we'll head to the center." He turned and headed back toward town, soon joining a line of cars pouring into the parking near the center.

He found a spot, leashed up Barney, and she snuggled Sunny close to her. He nodded as he slipped out of the car and raced around to open her door. She slid out and he wrapped an arm around her as they hurried to the door.

They got inside and she shook the rain from her hair, still careful to keep a hold on Sunny.

Sara greeted them. "There you two are. Good. I'll put your names down. Charlotte just got here with Ben. They're already inside. Go on in. There are blankets and towels so you can dry off."

Robin was glad to hear Charlotte had made it safely here, too. She followed Jay and Barney into the main room of the center and soon they were swallowed up by the crowd of townsfolk.

They dried off and Lillian came hurrying up to them. "I checked with Sara, and Etta isn't here. Have you seen her? Maybe she slipped in without Sara getting her name down?"

"Haven't seen her."

"I sent Zoe to search the crowd. I'm

worried about her. She lives alone. But surely she got the alert." The worry was clear in Lillian's eyes.

Just then Zoe and Mason came up to them. "I've looked everywhere. I don't see her."

Robin thought for a moment. "You know, I think I saw the light on at the historical society as we drove past. That's kind of unusual, isn't it? She would have closed it up and gone home. Though maybe she just forgot and left a light on."

"I tried calling her, but I didn't get an answer. She hadn't made any plans to leave the island last time I talked to her." Lillian turned and searched the crowd again.

"Let me go check the historical society building," Jay said. "If she's not there, I'll run to her house."

"I hate to have you go out in this." Lillian frowned.

"Won't take long," Jay assured her.

"I'll go with you," Mason offered. "Just in case you need help."

Jay kissed Robin quickly and handed her the leash. "Here, take Barney. I'll be back soon."

"Stay safe." She frowned, not pleased that he was going back out into the storm. But someone really did need to check on Etta, and of course, Jay wanted to help allay Lillian's worries.

Mason turned to Zoe. "I'll be back. You stay here. Stay safe."

Zoe nodded but didn't look very pleased that Mason was heading out into the storm, either.

"Ready?" Jay asked.

Mason nodded.

She and Zoe stood side by side and watched as the men left. Jay knew how to be careful. He'd be fine. Just fine. But still, an uneasiness slithered through her. She turned to Zoe, a reassuring smile plastered on her face. "They'll be fine."

"Right. I'm sure they will." But Zoe's voice sounded as uncertain as hers did.

CHAPTER 12

"We'll take my car." Jay led the way to where he'd gotten a parking spot at the far edge of the lot. The rain poured down, drenching them, and his clothes stuck to him as they hurried along.

Mason grabbed his arm. "Look. The entrance to the parking lot is flooded and a tree fell across the drive."

Jay looked over and let out a sigh. "Looks like no one is getting in or out of this lot anytime soon. It's only a couple of blocks. You up for a quick jog over there?"

"Not seeing we have a choice."

He and Mason jogged through the pelting rain, sloshing through puddles and trying to avoid the flooded areas on the streets. They got to the historical society and Jay tried the door. It swung open easily. "Etta?" He called out as they pushed inside, dripping water everywhere.

"Etta?" He tried again, louder, so his voice could be heard over the howling winds.

"I hear something back that way." Mason pointed.

They hurried down a hallway. "Etta?" He called out again.

"Back here. Help."

They rushed into a back room and stopped. A large bookcase had tumbled over, and there, pinned under it, was Etta.

"Oh, Jay. Thank goodness. I didn't know when anyone would come to find me. I'm stuck and can't get out. And of course, I didn't have my phone on me. I was trying to put some documents up on the top shelf to keep them safe if we get flooding and then the whole bookcase fell before I could get away from it."

"We'll get you out. Don't worry." He surveyed the damage, trying to figure out how to move the case without causing more harm.

Mason walked up beside him. "We need to prop that end up. Move those boxes so they don't fall, then we'll lift this end off of her."

Jay glanced and saw that Mason had come up with a good plan. He nodded as they sprang into action. "Okay, Etta, you ready? We're going to lift this off of you and then you try to crawl out."

"Okay."

They lifted the heavy wooden bookcase and he saw Etta try to get loose.

"I can't. I'm still stuck."

"I'll go prop that end up more. We'll try again." Mason went over to work on finding something to help stabilize the end of the case.

Jay bent down near Etta. "Don't worry. We'll get you out of here. Everything is going to be just fine."

Etta nodded but he couldn't help but notice how pale she looked.

"Okay, let's try this again." Mason returned and they leveraged up the bookcase and he slid a wooden box under it.

Jay reached down, gently took hold of Etta, and helped her slide free. He stood to help her to her feet.

"Watch out," Mason called as the case began to totter.

Jay grabbed Etta and hurled them both backward, just as the bookcase crashed to the floor. He and Etta landed in a clump on the floor, inches away from the bookcase.

"You okay?" He looked at her closely.

"Yes... I'm just glad you found me."

"We'll help you up."

He rose and he and Mason reached down for Etta. She tried to stand, but he could see the pain on her face. "My ankle. I don't think..."

"Not a problem. We'll just carry you to the community center. You're going to get wet, but you'll be fine."

She nodded.

He gently lifted her in his arms. "Clear the way, will you, Mason?"

Mason moved some boxes and cleared a pathway to the door. He looked at Mason as they stood in the doorway to the building. It was almost impossible to see through the sheets of rain. "Stay close. We don't want to get turned around in this."

Mason nodded. "Hey, you're the one who knows the town. I'll be stuck like glue to you, buddy."

"Don't forget to close the door," Etta said.

Jay chuckled. "No, ma'am. We won't."

Lillian paced back and forth, waiting for news about Etta. She tried to busy herself delivering hot coffee to the stranded townsfolk, but her mind was filled with reasons why Etta wasn't here now. And none of the reasons were good ones.

She walked over to the door to check with Sara, just in case Etta had arrived and she'd missed her. Sara looked up at her from the check-in desk and just shook her head, no.

The door swung open again and Lillian looked hopefully in its direction. But it was Delbert Hamilton ushering Camille inside. "Come on, honey. Let's get you inside and dried off."

"But I don't want to sit here with a bunch of strangers." Camille's voice came out in a petulant whine.

"They aren't strangers. They are the people who live here. We know most of them. And we can't get off the island now. You heard the bridge was closed." He turned and smiled at Sara.

Sara smiled back at him. "I'll add you two to the list. Glad you made it here. The storm is taking a nasty turn toward us according to Sheriff Dave."

"We were going to ride out the storm at Camille's family's house, but then we got the alert to evacuate."

"And I, of course, needed to pack my essentials." Camille frowned. "But Delbert only let me bring two suitcases. Certainly not enough."

"Well, darlin', it took you quite a bit to just pack those up."

Camille walked a few steps over to the opening to the main room. "We're supposed to stay in there? With everyone? On... are those *cots*?"

"Not sure there are any cots left now. You're the last people to get here, I expect. The alert went out quite a while ago." Lillian looked at Camille, annoyed at the woman's attitude. Annoyed she was even here. Camille should be *grateful* the town had a safe place like this for people to come to now that the bridge was closed. But then, Camille was Camille. Always.

"I don't know why the weathermen got the forecast so wrong. If we'd known it was going to get this bad, we would have headed back home to Mama's house in Comfort Crossing."

"Hurricanes are unpredictable at best, Camille." Lillian tried to keep the irritation out of her voice. She was worried about Etta, and a little inconvenience wouldn't hurt Camille. *And* it wasn't like any of the other people here weren't going through the same inconveniences. Storms were tough on everyone.

Lillian sighed. *And,* she freely admitted, Camille got on her nerves.

"Well, you'd think they could predict better than this." Camille shook out her hair. "I need to dry off. Are there at least towels here? Or Delbert, go out and get my suitcase. I have a hairdryer in there."

"I'm sorry, Sheriff Dave wants people to stay inside once they get here." Sara looked at Delbert, not Camille.

Delbert took Camille's elbow. "Come on, let's see what we can find. Get you dried off and warm." He turned and smiled at Lillian. "We'll be fine."

"But Delbert, I need my things," Camille's eyes flashed with defiance.

"Later, darlin'" Delbert headed toward the main room with Camille letting out a streak of complaints the whole time.

Lillian turned to Sara. "I don't know why that man stays with her."

Sara laughed. "Good luck to Delbert

keeping her happy while held captive here at the center. She sounded like this storm was all his fault."

"I think I'll just keep a wide berth from her."

"Good plan."

Lillian headed off to the kitchen to see if The Yarnies needed more help passing out coffee and cookies, though she'd see if someone else would volunteer to bring it out to Delbert and Camille. She'd already hit her fill of the woman. She should go and check on Lucky, too. Make sure the pup was doing okay in the crowded center.

At least helping out in the kitchen and checking on the dog would keep her mind off of Etta.

Maybe.

Where *was* the woman? She couldn't help worrying about her.

ROBIN PACED AROUND inside the center waiting for Jay to return. She'd lost count of how many times she'd glanced at her watch. Barney walked by her side as she juggled the kitten in her other arm.

Zoe walked up to her. "Any sign of them?"

"No, not yet."

"Want me to watch your kitten while you walk Barney around?"

"That would be great." She handed Sunny over to Zoe. "Sunny. Her name is Sunny."

Zoe stroked the kitten as it settled into her arms, purring. Zoe laughed. "She's a noisy little thing."

"She's a purr monster, that's for sure. The storm and the hubbub haven't seemed to bother her one bit."

"I'll watch her while you give Barney some exercise."

"Thanks, Zoe. Let me know if you see the guys come back." She walked away, out of the main room of the center and down a long hallway, trying to escape some of the crowd. Barney was beginning to look a bit anxious. Whether it was the storm or the crowd, she wasn't sure. She circled twice around inside the center and ended up by the front door yet again.

Sara looked up from the table and shrugged. "Sorry, they're not back yet."

"I hope they found Etta and I wish they'd get back here." She didn't know how many more laps around the place she could do before she went crazy with worry.

"I'm sure they're fine," Sara said encouragingly.

"I'm sure you're right." But she *wasn't* sure. She still had this nagging feeling and just wanted to lay her eyes on Jay and know he was okay. Then maybe she'd feel better. Or some better. The storm had her on edge. She let out a long breath, trying to steady her nerves.

The door swung open and a group of people entered, crowding through the door, trying to get in out of the storm.

With all the commotion, Barney tugged on the leash unexpectedly and pulled it right from her hand. She lunged for the leash but wasn't quick enough. Barney rushed past the people and headed toward the door. "Barney, come back."

She pushed through the people to get to the door and to her dismay, the dog rushed out into the storm. She whirled toward Sara. "I have to get Barney. He got out."

"No, don't go out in that." Sara jumped up from her chair.

"I have to." Her heart pounding, she raced out into the storm just in time to catch a glimpse of Barney running across the parking lot, his leash trailing behind him.

She had to catch him. *Had to.* Or Mrs. Gleason would never forgive her.

And Jay probably wouldn't either...

CHAPTER 13

Jay and Mason hurried through the storm. Jay tried to shield Etta as best he could from the drenching rain. But at least they'd found Etta and they were getting her to safety. They finally made it to the community center and Mason battled against the wind to open the door. Jay maneuvered through, careful not to bump Etta's hurt ankle.

Lillian and Zoe came rushing up to them. "You found her. Oh, Etta, are you okay?" Lillian's eyes were full of concern.

"She's hurt her ankle. Looks pale." Jay set Etta down carefully and she leaned against him. He wrapped an arm around her waist to steady her.

Lillian touched Jay's arm. "Thank you so much for going and finding her."

"It was no problem." He was always glad to help Lillian after all she'd done for him.

"I saw Dr. Harden here. I'll go find her." Zoe sent a quick look at Mason as if checking to make sure he was really here and safe, then hurried away.

Gary showed up with a chair for Etta and she gratefully sat down.

"What happened?" Lillian asked.

"It was silly of me. I was stashing some records up high on the shelves, just in case there was any flooding. I climbed a ladder, but lost my balance and grabbed hold of the bookcase. The whole thing tumbled over. My leg was caught and I couldn't move the bookcase. It was too heavy. Luckily Jay and Mason found me and were able to get me free."

Ashley Harden hurried up to them, doctor bag in hand. "I hear Etta needs to be checked out."

"Ashley, yes. Etta was trapped under a bookcase." Lillian hovered over Etta.

"It's my ankle."

Ashley checked out Etta as Jay's gaze

roamed the room, looking for Robin. He turned to Lillian. "Have you seen Robin?"

"No, not for a bit. I'm sure she's here in the crowd somewhere."

He noticed Zoe was holding Sunny. "You have her kitten?"

Zoe smiled and petted the kitten. "I'm just holding her for Robin. Last I saw Robin she was walking Barney around."

He scanned the crowded room yet again and frowned. He just wanted to set his sights on her. See her. He really wanted to kiss her or hug her, but he'd settle with just seeing her smile.

Sara came rushing up to them and grabbed his arm. "Jay, there you are. You have to find her."

"Robin?" Concern swept through him at the sound of panic in Sara's voice.

"Yes. She was walking Barney near the doorway and a group of people came in. Barney got away from her and ran out the door. I tried to stop her but she... she ran out after him."

"She went out in this storm?" Now his own voice was filled with panic, and fear gripped his heart.

Sara nodded.

Jay whirled toward the door. "I've got to find her."

"Jay, you can't go back out there." Lillian reached out to stop him. "Not now. It's gotten too dangerous out there."

"I have to." He had no choice. He had to find her. Make sure she was okay. Why had she gone out in this storm? Why?

He knew why. There's was no way she'd let Barney fend for himself out in the storm.

His heart pounded in his chest, strangling him, as he rushed back out into the furious storm.

ROBIN RACED through the wind and rain, drenched, as she chased after Barney. The dog managed to keep about a half-block ahead of her no matter how hard she struggled to catch up to him.

Then suddenly, she lost sight of him.

No!

She pulled up short and looked to the left and the right, uncertain which way to head. She couldn't just leave him out here in the storm, but how could she find him when she could barely see through the pouring rain? She swiped at the water rolling down her face. Her clothes stuck to her like a second skin.

She called out to him. "Barney. Barney, where are you?" Not that she really thought the dog would turn around and come to her...

If he could even hear her.

She had to find him, though. Mrs. Gleason.

She couldn't bear to think of telling Mrs. Gleason she'd lost the dog. And if truth be told, even if the dog annoyed her with his uncanny ability to destroy her shoes, she had grown pretty fond of him.

Then, suddenly she knew...

She twirled around and raced off through the rain.

CHAPTER 14

Jay darted under an overhang by a storefront on Main Street and tried to call Robin. No cell service. Not surprising in a storm like this, but annoying. He shoved the phone back in his pocket. He had to find Robin.

But *how* was he going to find her? Barney could have gone anywhere, and Robin was out there somewhere racing after the dog. He never should have left Barney with Robin. He never should have left Robin's side during the storm. But then, he *had* to go look for Etta for Lillian.

Pure frustration surged through him mixed in with a healthy dose of fear.

He peered through the sheets of rain, straining for any sign of Robin. Any sign of Barney. A broken branch skipped down the street in the violent wind, dancing a jig with a smashed and tattered box. It was dangerous out here with debris whipping around in the wind.

Fear knotted his insides as he swept a hand up to shove his dripping hair from his face. If anything happened to Robin...

He took off at a steady jog but afraid he might be going in the exact wrong direction. "Robin!" He yelled against the howling wind, but the wind just tossed his call back to him, mocking him. Hammering home how hopeless it was.

Then it came to him.

He knew where Barney would have gone. He spun around and headed back in the other direction, praying that he was right. Hoping he'd find both Robin and Barney there.

ROBIN BENT over against the wind as she fought her way along the street. She screamed when a palm branch flashed past her, whipping her with its fronds. But she couldn't stop now. She couldn't.

She struggled along the sidewalk on the last half block, doubled over against the wind, and prayed she was right. She almost cried in relief as she battled her way up to the front of Mrs. Gleason's bungalow.

And there he was.

Barney. Huddled against the front door.

Thank goodness.

She dropped to her knees beside the dog and hugged him. The dog shook in her arms. "Sh, it's okay. I've got you now. It will be okay." Grabbing hold of the leash—very firmly—she looked over at her bungalow, then out at the storm.

There was no way she could make it back to the community center now. The winds were too strong and it was too dangerous. They needed to seek shelter. She'd have to take cover in her bungalow and hope for the best.

She scooped Barney up in her arms and slowly made her way against the wind and over to her front porch. Even just going that far exhausted her. She set him down by the front door, the leash still firmly wrapped around her hand. Twice.

She didn't have her key but knew that Charlotte had hidden one under a rock in the heavy planter beside the door. Charlotte was always forgetting her keys. Thank goodness for good old forgetful Charlotte.

She grabbed the key, all the while making sure to keep a firm clasp on Barney's leash. She unlocked the door and hurried inside with Barney, tugging the door closed behind her.

She flipped on the switch... but nothing. She let out a sigh of frustration. The electricity was out. Not surprising. "Come on, Barney, let's find the battery lantern and get some light in here." It was somehow comforting to hear her voice and have someone... even Barney... to talk to.

She went to the kitchen, found the lantern, and flipped it on. That was better. Then she went to grab towels and dried Barney... who surprisingly let her do it. Then she wrapped a towel around herself, shivering. Whether from the chill or the edge of fear, she wasn't certain. With Barney in tow, she headed to her closet for dry clothes, all the while ignoring the howling wind and the fact that she was here in her bungalow. All alone. Riding out the storm with only Barney for companionship.

What if the roof blew off?

Or the bungalow flooded?

She ignored those thoughts and concentrated on getting into dry clothes.

She pulled on dry sweatpants and a sweatshirt, hoping they would chase away the chill. "Okay, Barney. What do you say we go out in the front room?" Somehow talking out loud to Barney helped chase away the in-this-all-alone fear that clutched at her.

She grabbed his leash, still clipped onto his collar. She just wasn't ready to let him loose. Not even in her house.

They padded back to the front room and she put the lantern on the coffee table all the while trying to talk herself out of a full-on panic.

"Don't worry, Barney. It's going to be fine." But even she could hear the doubt in her voice. The wind howled and rattled the shutters. She clasped her arms tightly across her chest. She didn't consider herself a weak woman, but she was scared. Very scared.

The storm was flaunting its power. Letting her know who was boss.

She wished more than anything that she and Barney were back in the community center and she was safe in Jay's arms.

CHAPTER 15

Jay could hardly stand upright against the strengthening wind. He didn't even bother to try to wipe away the rain coursing down his face. How in the world had Robin fought all this?

Or had she? Had she holed up somewhere? Was she hurt somewhere? Was she safe? Images of her trapped somewhere, pinned down by some fallen building, or worse yet... the power lines stretched across the island. Some still had power... maybe even some of them had been knocked to the ground just ready to electrocute anything in their path.

He chased away the thoughts, the frightening images. She had to be okay. She had to. He'd just realized how much he cared for her. He couldn't lose her.

He made his way along the streets, dodging debris that the storm kept tossing at him. At one point something hit his head and he felt warmth on his face. He was fairly certain blood was mingling with the rainwater on his forehead. He ignored it.

He turned the corner and struggled up to the porch of his destination. But he was wrong. No Barney. No Robin. He'd been sure he'd find them here at Mrs. Gleason's. But even if Robin had found Barney here, they couldn't have gotten inside.

He turned toward Robin's bungalow, his last hope. Then he saw it. Or thought he did. He slashed away the rain from his face.

Yes. He was certain. *Almost* certain. Or maybe it was hope more than certainty.

He peered through the storm. No, a faint glow *was* filtering out through the clear hurricane shutter on her front window.

She must be there. His heart thundered in his chest as he raced across to her bungalow, splashing through a river of water streaming between the two bungalows, and threw himself up her steps. He flung open the door to her screams.

"Sh, Robin. It's okay. It's me." Relief surged through him. He'd found her. And Barney was by her side. She was here. She was safe.

He rushed over and pulled her to her feet, gathering her into his arms. "Oh, Robs. You're here." He just as quickly set her away from him, looking her over carefully, his gaze going from head to toe. "Are you okay?"

She nodded. "I'm so glad to see you." She crumbled back into his arms.

He held her tight against him, never wanting to let her go. The hammering in his chest slowed. Somewhat. He felt her tremble in his arms, and his heart cracked just a little as he fought back images of what could have happened to her. He stroked her back, trying to soothe her. Or soothe himself. It all just entwined together. He finally spoke into her hair. "I was so frightened when I heard you went out in this storm. What were you thinking?"

"I was thinking Mrs. Gleason would kill me if Barney got lost."

He looked down and saw that she still held Barney's leash in her hand. "So, you found him."

"He was at Mrs. Gleason's."

"I thought he might go there." Jay set Robin away again, but rubbed his hands up and down her arms, making sure she was real.

She reached out to touch his face. "You're hurt."

"What?" He reached up and touched the tender spot on his temple and saw his hand come back with blood. "Yes, something hit me. It's crazy out there. Trash, signs, branches. Everything getting tossed around in the wind. Not sure what it was that did this."

"Come into the kitchen and let me get you cleaned up."

He could tell by her voice that she needed to do this, so even though he didn't think the wound was worth bothering over, he nodded and followed her into the kitchen. Barney trotted along beside them keeping right by their feet. "Not liking the storm much, huh, buddy? I'm with you. I'm not very fond of it myself." He reached down and petted the dog. He worried about sitting out the storm at the bungalow instead of the relative safety of the center, but nothing could be done about that now. They couldn't chance going out in the storm again. But he wasn't going to mention his concerns to Robin. He did his best to put on a confident, not-worried-about-a-thing look on his face.

He sat down at the table as Robin commanded and let her clean up and bandage his temple. Her hands were shaking as she did it, but he didn't mention that either.

"Okay, now we need to get you dried off. Why don't you take off your wet clothes? I've got some large t-shirts that I like to sleep in. You can wear one of those. And maybe just wrap in a towel?"

"Will have to do for now." He stood and shucked off his wet shirt.

ROBIN TRIED NOT to stare at Jay's chest. It's not like she hadn't seen it before. They'd gone to the beach. They'd gone swimming. But his chest glistened in the low lantern light and she saw every hard, defined muscle of his abs.

A towel. She was supposed to be getting him

a towel. And a t-shirt. Though, a shirt would cover those abs of his...

She shoved Barney's leash into Jay's hands. "I'll be right back."

She returned with two towels and he used one to dry off. Then shook out his hair.

"You going to watch me take off my shorts, too?" He cocked his head.

"I... um... No, I'm going to make some tea. I keep a small camp stove burner here and I want some tea." She turned and dug into a lower cabinet and took out the small stove, filled a tea kettle with water, and turned on the burner. When she finished, she turned back to Jay.

He had pulled on the t-shirt, covering his chest. Too bad. He'd also wrapped a towel firmly around his waist. She swallowed and looked away.

He walked up to her and laughed, wrapping his arms around her. "You like what you see?"

She grinned. "I sure do." She leaned against him, so glad to have his arms around her. Now the storm seemed not quite as scary. There was a time there, out in the storm, fighting the wind... well, she hadn't been sure she'd make it to safety, much less find Barney. Now, here she was, in Jay's arms.

Something hit the side of the house and she jumped. Jay pulled her closer. "It's going to be okay, Robs. I'm here. We're going to be fine."

She only hoped he was right.

CHAPTER 16

Zoe busied herself helping out at the center. Handing out blankets, bringing people cups of coffee, all the while holding Sunny tucked in one arm and occasionally searching the crowd to reassure herself that Mason was still here and hadn't run off on another dangerous escapade with Jay. Though, she was worried about Jay and Robin out in the storm. She hadn't seen them return.

Mason walked up to her, his arm full of blankets. "These are the last of them."

"I think there might be more in the old storage room. It's way in the back of the building. Let's go check."

The lights flickered, then came back on. "Oh, good. But maybe we should take a flashlight, just in case." They crossed over to a table of supplies and grabbed a flashlight. Mason followed her down a long hallway to the back of the building. The chatter of the crowd faded as they moved farther away.

She let out a long sigh. "Ah, the quiet is nice."

"It is."

The lights flickered again and she held her breath. But this time they didn't come on. She felt Mason take her hand and he flipped on the flashlight.

"I figured the electricity would go out eventually. Noah will start the generator now. But it will only run a few things. Some lights in the main room and the fridge. Let's get those blankets and get back there."

She led the way to the storage room and they opened the door. Mason swung the light in an arc around the room, aiming it at one side then the other.

"There." He pointed to the corner.

She juggled Sunny in one arm as they made their way over and dug through the stack of supplies. "I guess I should have given Sunny to someone else to watch. But I kind of like having her with me."

She twirled around at the sound of the door creaking closed behind them. "Oh, that startled me."

Mason held up the light to see the door then back to her. "So, since we're here all alone, mind if I sneak in a kiss?"

She didn't miss the playful look on his face. "You could probably do that."

Mason pulled her into his arms, leaned down, and kissed her gently. "Been wanting to do that for hours, but too many prying eyes around us."

She leaned against him, feeling his heartbeat. She could stay like this forever. But not really. They needed to get the blankets back to the main room. She sighed as she pulled away from him.

He snatched her back for one more quick kiss before they gathered up armfuls of blankets and headed back to the door. Mason juggled his armload while he wrestled with opening the door.

He set the lantern on a table by the door, dropped the blankets, and grappled with the door handle again. He slowly turned to her. "It doesn't seem to be working."

She dropped her armful of blankets and

handed Sunny to him. She turned the handle, leaned against the door, and turned it again, then pulled the door toward her and tried. Nothing.

"I... I think we're locked in here." She ignored the feeling of claustrophobia that crept through her just knowing they were locked in the small room.

Mason grabbed his phone. "Ah, no signal."

She took hers out. "Same. No signal."

"We could pound on the door and yell." Mason shrugged. "But no one is in this part of the building, and I doubt that anyone could hear it over the rain pouring on the roof. I never knew a metal roof could be so loud in a storm."

"I love the sound of a gentle rain on a metal roof, but when it really storms, it is loud."

"I guess we're stuck here for a bit."

"Someone will come looking for us eventually, right?" She looked at Mason for encouragement.

"They will. When your uncle doesn't see you for a while, he'll come looking."

"But we didn't tell anyone where we were headed." She chewed her bottom lip.

"I'm sure he won't let any corner of this building go unchecked." He raised the lantern, looking around the small room. "How about I pile up some blankets and we'll sit against the wall? Silly to just stand here."

She nodded as he handed Sunny back to her. He piled a generous stack of blankets up and motioned for her to come over. He sank down on the blankets and reached a hand up for her. She sat beside him and he circled an arm around her shoulder. "It's going to be okay. I'm sure Noah will come searching soon."

She leaned against him. "He will..."

She set Sunny on a stack of blankets beside her and the kitten pawed the blankets, then curled up in a ball.

"So, I know how we can keep busy until then." He grinned at her in the warm, low light of the lantern.

"What's that?"

"I'm thinking we could perfect our kissing."

She laughed, a bit of the tension easing out of her shoulders. "We could."

"It might take a while. We want to make sure we get it just right." The corners of his mouth twitched in a smile and she could see the hint of his dimple.

"Well, we should really work at perfecting it."

"We should." He leaned down and captured her lips with his.

Noah hurried around the center, checking on people, getting what they needed. He'd started the generator, but it was only set up to run a few lights in the building and the fridge in the kitchen. Darkness hovered in the corners, but most people had brought flashlights and lanterns with them and they were scattered around the room.

A group had set up in the corner playing cards, and he'd gotten them more lights for their tables. Another group had a jigsaw puzzle going, and he'd opened up a bin full of building blocks for a group of kids who were busy building forts with them, their play area illuminated by two bright battery operated lanterns.

The wind still howled outside as a testament to the raging storm outside the walls of the community center. At least they were safe in here. Or relatively safe. He glanced around at the crowded room. He *hoped* they were all safe here. It was too bad the bridge was closed and they couldn't all have gotten to the mainland.

Sara came up to him and pressed a cup of coffee into his hands. "Here, drink this. You've been going nonstop for hours." She kissed his cheek and smiled at him.

"I'm hoping the worst of the storm will soon be passing over us. I'm not getting a signal on my phone to see how it's tracking."

"Sherriff Dave came in a bit ago. He and his officers are staying inside here for a bit. Said it was too bad out there to continue their rounds. They'll head back out when the worst is over."

Noah scanned the room. "Have you seen Zoe? I haven't seen her in a while."

Sara frowned. "No. I haven't. Maybe she's in the kitchen?"

"Maybe. I think I'll go check. I'd just feel better if I can keep my eye on her. I know she's all grown up now, but old habits die hard."

"Go check then. And maybe sit down for a few minutes. You look exhausted."

He nodded but really had no plans to sit down. There was still too much to do. He hurried off to the kitchen and found Lillian and Dorothy there, but they hadn't seen Zoe in a while either. He frowned. It was silly to get worried. He knew she was here. Somewhere.

But where?

He turned around, left the kitchen, and started looking for Zoe in earnest. Soon, it was evident that no one had seen her in quite a while. He tried to steady his racing pulse. Of course, she was here, somewhere. She wouldn't go out in this. She knew better.

Didn't she?

But hadn't Robin run out after the dog? And no one had heard from her or Jay. He just hoped Jay had found Robin and they were holed up somewhere safe.

He hurried off to his office, hoping maybe she'd gone there for some peace and quiet. But the office was pitch dark and no Zoe.

Fear took hold of him. Where was his niece? Why hadn't he kept a better eye on her? He was running out of places to look for her.

Then he noticed the quiet. The winds had subsided. But he knew. It was just the eye of the storm passing over. They still had the backside of the storm to contend with. He hurried back to the front door to make sure no one headed outside.

CHAPTER 17

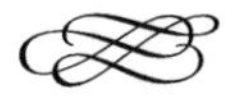

Robin slowly woke up, not sure where she was, or what had changed. Then as she opened her eyes, she realized. It was quiet now. The winds had died down. She fully opened her eyes and saw Jay was right there, holding her, a smile on his face.

"Hey, sleepyhead." His voice was low and soothing.

"I can't believe I fell asleep. How long was I out?" She blinked a few times, trying to clear her mind.

"Couple hours. Sounds like the worst of the storm has passed. The eye passed over and then it started in again. But now, I think it's lessening. Still can't get a signal on my phone to check, though."

"They should do the siren after the sheriff has had time to make rounds of the town and see if it's safe enough to go out. It might be awhile. Normally if we had evacuated it might be a day or so before we could come back. But with everyone stuck here on the island? I'm not sure what they'll do."

"I'm okay here with you." He reached over and pushed a lock of her hair away from her face. "Very okay." He leaned down and kissed her.

For a bit they sat there, kissing as she cuddled in his arms. He was right. She was okay with just being here with him.

Finally, though, she pushed off the couch, reluctant to leave Jay's arms but wanting to look outside. She peered through the window with the clear hurricane shutter but couldn't see out well enough. "I'm going to open the door and look out."

Jay stood and strode over. "I'll get it." He opened the door and slowly slid back the hurricane protection.

She peered around his shoulder. A steady rain pattered down from the sky, but the dark clouds overhead were already beginning to break up.

He turned back to her and smiled. "Looks like we made it through okay, Robs. I told you that we would."

She walked into his arms as they stood looking out into the soaked courtyard. "You did say that."

He let out a little chortle. "Well, I'm glad it came true. Would have hated to be lying to you."

ZOE WOKE UP, unsure of her surroundings in the pitch dark. She couldn't see a thing. Nothing.

Slowly she remembered. The storage room. But where was the lantern light?

She noticed the quiet, though. The pounding on the metal roof had turned into a gentle drumming.

She moved slightly, feeling trapped. Her legs were pinned. She struggled to put all her scrambled thoughts together.

Mason.

She and Mason were locked in the storage room. She moved again, feeling his strong arms tighten around her as she shifted. He mumbled something she didn't quite catch.

She wondered how long they'd been in here. Surely Uncle Noah would have been looking for them. She moved slowly, yet again, trying to disentangle herself from Mason. Though... he was very comfortable to rest against...

"You awake?" Mason's low voice drifted through the darkness.

"I am. Can't believe I fell asleep." On him. Tangled up with him.

"We didn't get much sleep last night with all the hubbub of the storm."

"How long have we been here?" She shifted against him, feeling the smooth texture of his shirt and the firm muscles of his arm.

"Not sure." He rustled beside her.

She reached out one hand, searching for her phone. It had been right next to her. You know, before she'd fallen asleep all tangled up with Mason. Her fingers slid over the face of her cellphone and she grasped it, turning it on.

"Two hours. We've been here two hours. Why hasn't Noah found us?"

"Maybe he's been too busy and hasn't noticed you're missing?"

"I don't know. That doesn't sound like Uncle Noah. More likely he's gone into a panic that he couldn't find me." She hated thinking about Noah all worried. "Now that it's not so noisy with the storm, maybe we should try pounding on the door. Maybe someone will hear us."

"We probably should." Mason agreed, but reached over and pulled her into his arms again. "Or, we could just stay here and kiss some more."

That didn't sound like a half-bad plan...

But, no. Noah would be worried. But, maybe just one kiss.

Which led to another kiss. And another.

Suddenly the door swung open and an arc of light cut through the room. "Zoe, thank goodness. I've been looking everywhere for you." Noah stood in the doorway, a lantern held high. "What are you doing? I've been so worried."

She hastily jumped up and struggled with straightening out her clothing and pulling back her hair, feeling like a teenager caught necking on the couch. "We came looking for more blankets and got locked in here."

She glanced over at Mason and his face held the same look as her feelings. Guilt at being caught kissing.

"It opened for me." Noah cocked his head.

Mason jumped up beside her. "No, sir. The door was locked. We tried everything."

"It is a bit tricky sometimes." Noah looked from her to Mason and back to her. "But you're okay?"

"I'm fine." She started to walk toward Noah, then turned around. "Wait, we need to find Sunny."

"Who?"

"Sunny. Robin's kitten. She's in here somewhere."

Noah held up the lantern and she spied Sunny stretching and arching her back on a pile of blankets, looking annoyed that they'd awakened her. She scooped up the kitten and turned to her uncle. "Has the storm passed?"

"It has. Just steady rain now. The sheriff went out a few minutes ago to check on things."

Mason gathered up a stack of blankets. "So, now what happens?"

"We wait until we get the all-clear that we can leave the center." Noah grabbed some of the blankets. "Let's head back to the main room. Still a lot to do."

She hurried after Noah and grabbed his arm. "I'm sorry to have worried you. I didn't mean to. We were just trying to help. Getting more blankets. Then that silly door just wouldn't budge."

Noah hugged her with one arm. "I know. I was just so worried that something had happened to you or you'd gone out in the storm. Didn't think of this old storage room until just a bit ago."

"Well, I'm glad you found us." And she was glad he wasn't mad at her. But, to be honest, was she glad they were found? It had been awfully nice all cuddled up alone with Mason...

CHAPTER 18

Lillian turned to Gary. "I wish the phones were working. I'm worried about Jay and Robin."

"I'm sure he found her and they're holed up somewhere, waiting for the all-clear."

"You're probably right." She stared at the phone, willing it to get a signal.

Noah, Zoe, and Mason came walking up.

"There you are," Lillian said. "Gary was wondering where you two got off to."

"We got locked in an old storage room, but Noah found us."

"You okay?" Lillian looked them over, but they looked fine. They looked... She smothered a smile. They looked more than fine. And she was pretty sure that was some whisker burn on

Zoe's cheek. *Looks like the two of them found a pleasant way to pass the time.*

She turned at the sound of the door opening. Sheriff Dave came in, shaking off water from his rain slicker as he entered. "Well, good news. Only found one downed power line out by the bridge. Hopefully, power can be restored soon. There's some localized flooding in our regular low spots. Looks like a few buildings have roof damage. Lots of branches down and a few trees are blocking some streets. We'll get those cleared up as quickly as possible."

"So it's okay to leave?" Lillian asked.

"You can go check on your businesses and homes. But there will be a curfew after sunset. We don't want people moving around in the dark until things get all cleared up. I've radioed about the bridge and we'll get that checked out soon. In the meantime, I'm trying to arrange for one of the ferries that goes to Whisper Island to shuttle from here to the mainland."

She turned to Gary. "I really want to go check on the inn."

"I'll go with you," Mason offered.

"Me, too. I can help." Zoe glanced at Noah. "Is that okay?"

Noah frowned slightly but nodded. "The center will stay open for those folks who need it. Some will probably stay until the electricity is back on."

"We'll all go together, then." Lillian turned back to the sheriff.

The sheriff held up a hand. "The lot is blocked off right now. We need to cut a downed tree that's blocking the entrance."

"We could walk," Lillian suggested.

"Still a pretty steady rain," the sheriff said.

"I'll get the chainsaw." Noah nodded and headed away.

"I'll help Noah, then we'll head out." Gary gave her a quick hug.

"I'll go check on Etta, but I'm anxious to get back to the inn."

She left the men to deal with the tree and went to find Etta. She was sitting up with her leg propped up on the chair across from her. "You feeling okay?" Lillian asked.

"Okay as can be expected. A little sore and bruised. Dr. Harden said to stay off my feet as much as possible."

"We're going to go head out and check on the inn. Are you going to be okay here?"

"I will. Noah said he'd send someone over

to check on my house. If it's okay, he said he'd drive me home."

"Are you sure you'll be okay at home?"

"I'll be fine."

"Okay, but I'll check on you."

Etta nodded. "Thanks, Lillian."

Lillian turned and headed back to the front door, hoping the men had cleared the tree and they could go to the inn. She just hoped the inn had survived without much damage.

She looked at her cell phone again. Still no service. They needed to find Jay and Robin, too. Jay was resourceful, and she hoped they were fine, but she wouldn't take a deep breath until she knew for sure.

JAY SLIPPED on his still-damp shorts, contemplating jogging to his house and getting some dry clothes as soon as it was safe to do so. He opened the door and walked out into the gentle rain just as Sheriff Dave pulled his car up in front of the bungalow. The sheriff rolled down his window when Jay approached.

"There are going to be lots of people glad to see you, Jay. Robin with you?"

"She is. We holed up at her bungalow. Couldn't make it back to the community center by the time I found her."

"Did she find Mrs. Gleason's missing pup?"

"She did."

"They've given the all-clear for people to go out and check on their property, but we have a sunset to sunrise curfew in place. Be careful if you go out."

"Will do. I'll go check my place, then head over to the inn and see if Lillian needs anything."

The sheriff nodded, rolled up his window, and pulled away. Jay trotted back inside the bungalow.

"Robs? We can leave now. I want to go check my house, then go check on the inn."

Robin came walking out of the kitchen looking impossibly adorable with tousled hair, loose t-shirt, and bare feet. Not to mention she was right here where he could see her, not out in the storm with him frantically searching for her. He couldn't resist it. He pulled her into his arms.

She leaned against him. "We should bring Barney with us. He's still kind of shaken up by the storm."

"Good idea," Jay agreed as he reluctantly let her go.

"But leash him up. The last thing we want is to go chasing after him again."

They closed up the bungalow and walked over to Jay's house, avoiding the clumps of fallen branches, broken items that had been tossed about in the storm, and the areas of deeper pools of water. Barney walked along beside them but didn't look very happy about it.

Jay checked out his house, pleased to see that except for the messy yard, it looked like everything was intact. He put on dry clothes and found Robin standing by the window, looking out over the bay. "It looks almost peaceful out there now, doesn't it?"

He came up behind her and slipped an arm around her waist. "It does. And the rain has stopped now."

"It looks like the sun is trying to come out, too."

"All that's left is the cleanup."

"Until the next storm. I never really get used to this. We were lucky this time." She leaned against him and he took in her warmth, balancing her against his side. She belonged there. Next to him. A surge of gratefulness swept through him. For the fact they'd finally realized what they meant to each other, for the fact that he'd found her safe from the storm, and for... well, for the opportunity to just stand here by her side, holding her.

They stood like that for a few minutes, enjoying the peace, before he let her go. "I think we'll take Barney with us to the inn. Lil won't mind. I don't think he's ready to be left alone."

"I don't think he is either." Robin nodded.

He clipped the leash back on Barney and they headed out to the inn. They passed a few people on the street who waved as they hurried to go check on their homes and businesses. He heard a chain saw in the distance and someone nailing something further down the road. The familiar sounds of Belle Island awakening from the aftermath of a storm.

They got to the inn and entered, hearing voices coming from further inside. "Lillian?" he called out.

Lillian hurried up to him and gave him a hug, then released him and smothered Robin with a hug. "You're here. You're both okay?"

"We're fine." Robin hugged Lil back. "Jay found me and we stayed at my bungalow. The storm had gotten too bad to get back to the center. There was no cell service so I couldn't let anyone know we were okay."

"And I see you found Barney." Lillian nodded at the dog.

"We did. He'd gone back to Mrs. Gleason's."

"Well, I'm just glad you're okay."

"How's the inn?" he asked as he ran his glance around the main room.

"We've just started checking. Mason and Zoe went up to the top floor and they're checking each room. Gary and I are checking things out down here. We have a bit of water leaking in the kitchen. Through that old window. You know the one? We need to replace it."

"I'll go check in there and get things cleaned up."

He and Robin headed to the kitchen. He propped open the door from the dining room to the kitchen and told Barney to sit there. The dog sat in the middle of the opening and didn't take his eyes off them as they looked around the kitchen.

He checked on the generator, and thankfully it had come on automatically and the fridge was running, so no loss of food. Hopefully, the electric would come back on soon, though sometimes it took days after a storm for it to be restored.

He cleaned up the water on the floor and looked around. Everything seemed fine. Lillian and Gary came into the kitchen with Zoe and Mason following behind.

"Robin, there you are. You're okay?" Zoe rushed up to them. "I have Sunny up in my room. She's sleeping on my pillow last I checked."

"Thank you for taking care of her." Robin smiled.

"Looks like we were really lucky. We'll have lots of clean up on the property. Lots of branches and palm fronds down. The sand has covered the walkway to the beach. Lost a palm tree, too." Lillian bustled further into the kitchen. "But now. How about we scrounge up some food for everyone?"

"Let me make it," he offered.

"I'll go grab a table. We can eat out on the deck. We might even have a pretty sunset now that the storm has passed," Gary said.

"Let me help you," Mason offered, and he and Gary headed out.

"You two go do whatever. I'll get some food

made. Will have to be sandwiches, but at least we'll eat." He shooed Lillian and Robin away.

He went and took off two of the hurricane shutters and light poured into the kitchen. Much better. He looked around the kitchen with a critical eye. He loved this space. His space. Okay, technically it was Lillian's kitchen, but it felt like his. Felt like home. And he was glad to be back in it. Alone. Working in it. He couldn't wait for the inn to open, fill with people, and for life to get back to normal.

He strode over to the fridge and pulled out food, ready to make a feast. Was everyone as starved as he was?

CHAPTER 19

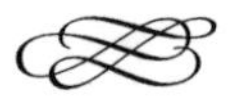

Zoe looked around at her friends sitting at the table, enjoying the feast Jay had made. She looked down at her plate, piled with food. Couldn't help it. Between the stress and the storm and every other excuse she could think of, she was famished and she'd freely admit it to anyone.

Mason sat next to her, smiling at her occasionally in the midst of the friendly banter about the table. Lillian made plans for the cleanup and they all offered to help her tomorrow. Robin sat with Sunny on her lap, petting the purring kitten who seemed oblivious she'd survived a hurricane. Barney lazed on the deck, keeping an eye on them, while Lucky slept under the table.

Mason squeezed her hand under the table, and she laced her fingers through his. She could almost believe that this was real life. That she lived back here on the island. That Mason was part of her life here. That...

... that things weren't going to dissolve into nothingness when she headed back home and Mason headed to Seattle.

She pushed the thoughts away and concentrated on what Jay was saying as he stood. "Robin and I should go. Got to beat the curfew. We'll head back to my house."

Robin looked at Jay with a questioning glance.

"You'll stay with me while the electricity is out?" Jay said it more as a question than a statement. "Won't you?"

"That's probably a good idea. Even if the town will gossip." Robin nodded slowly.

"Pshaw. Since when do we let a little town gossip stop us from anything? Smart idea to stay with Jay for a bit while things settle down," Lillian said. "You two head out and get back home before sunset. We'll clear this all up."

"We'll be back first thing in the morning." Jay took Robin's hand as she stood with Sunny tucked in her arms. They walked down the steps of the deck and disappeared around the corner.

A small smile played across the corners of Lillian's lips as she watched them leave. "About time they realized they love each other."

Zoe stared after where they'd disappeared. They really were a great couple. So in sync and it was obvious to everyone how in love they were. A tad bit of jealousy swept through her. She'd never had that with anyone. That complete connection.

"You okay?" Mason interrupted her thoughts. "You look deep in thought."

"I'm... I'm fine." But was she?

She and Mason stayed with Lillian and Gary on the deck, watching the sunset. Soft colors painted the sky in delicate shades of yellow and pink, mocking the violent skies of earlier today.

They all finally rose and carried the dishes back inside. "Gary and I have the dishes tonight. And Jay's comment about Robin staying with him got me thinking. I think you two should move into the Grand Suite. It's two bedrooms. I'd feel better if Zoe wasn't in her room alone with no electricity. Does that work for you two?"

"I... uh..." She turned to look at Mason.

"I think that's a great idea. We'll collect our things and move." Mason turned to her. "If that's okay with you?"

"Sure, that's fine." It was fine, wasn't it? They could have a nice evening together. And she hadn't exactly been thrilled about spending the night in the dark room all alone.

"Let's go to my office and I'll grab you the key."

They headed to Lillian's office and she flipped the light switch and laughed. "Oops, force of habit. I've got a flashlight lantern on the desk." She crossed over and soon the room was softly illuminated by the light.

Zoe noticed a frown on Lil's face. "Everything okay?"

"Yes... I just..." Lillian slowly looked around the room. "It must be just the flashlight. Something feels off." She shook her head and reached into the drawer. "Here's a key that will work on the suite. It's at the other end of the hall from where your rooms are. If you look in the storage room, there's a cart you can use to move your things."

"Thanks so much for this." Mason took the key.

"I should be thanking you two for all the help you've given me with the inn." Lillian walked out of the office and handed the flashlight to Mason. "Now you two go on and have yourself a nice night."

Zoe was suddenly tired and ready to settle in for the evening. They headed to the lobby while Lillian disappeared back toward the kitchen.

Mason shone the light across the main room. Darkened corners lurked around them from the shuttered windows.

"I'll have to help Dad take down the shutters tomorrow. Still looks like a horror movie set in here tonight."

Mason threaded an arm around her as they walked through the lobby and up the stairs. He got the cart and they piled their things on it before they headed to the new suite.

She stepped inside as he held up the light. "Oh... it's so nice." The sitting area had a couch and two chairs and a painting of a walkway to the beach. There was a kitchenette in one corner. Two doors, one on each side of the room, led to the two bedrooms.

"I'm going to see if I can open up the covering on the French doors to the balcony." Mason opened the door and wrestled with the hurricane covering until the night sky finally was visible. He swung them wide, letting in the fresh night air.

"That's so much better. I hate the closed-up rooms in a hurricane."

He turned to her with an impish grin. "I don't know. I had a pretty good time in that closed-up storage room."

The heat of a blush crossed her face. "Okay, that one closed-up room wasn't so bad."

"I brought the red wine I had in my other room. Want some?"

"That sounds nice."

"At least it doesn't need ice and doesn't need to be chilled."

"Truth." She wandered over to the couch and watched while he poured the wine and lit a couple of candles. He set the candles on the coffee table, then went to rescue the wine. The candles sent dancing, flickering shadows against the wall.

He settled next to her and handed her a glass. "To surviving my first hurricane."

She gently touched her glass to his. "To surviving yet *another* hurricane."

"I have to say, I'm not a huge fan of them." He smiled wryly.

"I guess you kind of get used to them. The first few we had when Noah and I first moved here? Those sent me into a tizzy. But then finally it just becomes a way of life. An annoying one, but it's just life down here."

"When did you move here?"

"I was fairly young. Noah and I vacationed here and loved it. We needed a change. So he left everything behind to move me here." She shrugged. "He's given up so much for me. He left everything behind in Boston when he heard my parents died. Moved to Philadelphia. Poor guy trying to figure out how to raise a heartbroken little girl. But we figured it out eventually. He's... well, he's wonderful. I'm lucky he'd give up so much for me."

"I'm sorry about your parents." He reached over and took her hand.

She stared down at their entwined fingers for a moment, then back to his face. The face that held a sympathetic look in his eyes. "Thanks. It was hard. Still is sometimes. There are just some things a girl wants to share with her mother. But Noah did everything possible to make sure I had everything I needed. And I loved growing up here." She took a sip of her wine. "How about you? Have you always lived in Seattle?"

"I have. I like it there. Mostly. Traffic is crazy and the cost of living is ridiculous and keeps climbing."

"Does your mom live there, too?"

"When she's not off traveling somewhere for work. My folks were both workaholics. I think that was the demise of their marriage. They both put more effort into their jobs than their relationship." He looked at her. "You were very lucky to have Noah. Someone so interested in your life and taking care of you. I... well, I didn't have that. I was an inconvenience to Mom, and Dad was... well, clueless when it comes to kids and didn't try to fix that fact. But Dad and I have a pretty good relationship now. We've worked things out."

"I'm glad." Mason and Gary did seem like they were close now. Not as close as she was with Noah, but still, close.

Mason shrugged. "Don't see Mom much, so that much hasn't changed. I think some people just weren't meant to be parents." He gave her a little smile. "But I turned out okay."

"So, after being raised like that, do you want to have kids? You know, someday?" Why was she asking him that? It wasn't any of her business. But she knew that she wanted kids. Lots of them. She'd always wanted a brother or sister when she was growing up.

"I don't know. Maybe. Not sure what kind of parent I'd be. Didn't have the best role models. But I have learned from my folks. I don't let my job consume my life." He laughed. "I try at least."

And she didn't want to ask the next question, but she did anyway. "You probably have to get back to Seattle soon, don't you? I mean we don't even have cell service for you to call your work, and the electric is out so no wi-fi service."

"Yes, I have to figure that out. I'm hoping for at least cell service tomorrow. Or maybe get over to the mainland if they have service there."

"If they get the ferry going tomorrow. I bet they will. We'll need supplies delivered here for repairs."

He looked at her, searching her face. "But I'll tell you one thing, Zoe. I'm going to miss you when I head back home."

Her heart flipped and she steadied her wine glass, concentrating on the rim of the glass like it was the most interesting thing in the world.

She was going to miss him, too. They'd been wrapped up in this strange world the last few days. Weeks, actually. Ever since he'd come to town for Lillian and Gary's wedding. Then all the hurricane prep and waiting out the storm.

Soon they'd both be going back to real life. Soon.

But for now? For now, she wasn't going to think about that. She'd just enjoy the time she had left with him.

Sometimes a person who seemed so right came into your life at the wrong time. Or in the wrong place.

He tilted her face up and kissed her gently, then pulled back. "Will you miss me?"

She reached out and touched the light shadow of whiskers on his face. "I will miss you. I've had a really good time getting to know you."

"And I've had a good time getting to know you, too. Bet I'd get to know you better if I kissed you again."

"I bet you would." She grinned as he leaned over and settled his lips on hers.

CHAPTER 20

The next morning Zoe awoke and stretched out her arms. She hauled herself up in bed, confused for a moment until she remembered she was in the suite at the inn. She could hear Mason rummaging around in the main room.

She jumped out of bed and hurried to get dressed, deciding her hair was hopeless and pulling it back as best she could. She went out into the main room and a sudden shyness slipped over her. It felt so strangely intimate to be here with Mason, alone in the suite.

He turned to her and gave her a wide smile. "Morning, sleepyhead."

"I guess I was tired." She rarely slept this late. It was almost nine.

"Guess what. I've got good news."

"What's that?"

He walked over to the door and flipped a light switch. "Electricity came on."

"That was quick."

"Well, at least it's on here at the inn. And... I've got a little surprise for you."

"You do?"

He laughed and headed to the kitchenette. "Coffee."

She crossed over and gratefully took the mug from him. "That's fabulous. Couldn't ask for a better surprise."

"And what would you say if I said I had cinnamon rolls, too?"

"I'd say you were my hero." She grinned at him.

"Ha, then I'm your hero." He pulled two rolls out of the small microwave. "Jay had made these and gave me some when I went downstairs looking for coffee. I have to say, he looked quite pleased with himself puttering around that kitchen."

"So, maybe Jay's my hero." She smothered a smile.

"Ouch, you crush me." His eyes twinkled and he clutched at his heart.

"Okay, you can both be my hero."

"I guess I can share the title." He winked. "Oh, and why don't you charge your phone, then it will be ready if the cell service comes back?"

He was so practical. How could he have practical thoughts like that? All she wanted to think about was... his lips. How his shirt stretched across his broad shoulders. How... Nope, she was going to be practical, too. She hurried to her room, grabbed her charger, and plugged in her phone.

They went outside and sat at a small table he'd moved back out to the balcony. She relished the fresh air and sunshine.

They bantered back and forth like old friends. Or like... a real couple. Or something. But all the while, the nagging reality that he'd be leaving soon hovered over her. Tapping her on the shoulder. Taunting her with don't-get-to-used-to-this thoughts.

"I'm going to help Dad take down the hurricane shutters and tackle cleaning up the property."

He interrupted her thoughts. Her crazy thoughts.

"I'll see what Lillian wants me to do." She

heard her phone ding. "Oh, service must be back." She jumped up and went to look at her phone. A text from Noah, checking on her. She quickly texted him back that she was fine and she'd see him later today.

She went back out to the balcony and sat back down. A young woman walked on the beach with two young kids running in circles around her. The skies were clear and bright blue, but a wind blew the palm trees in a slow, swaying dance.

"It really is nice here on the island." Mason leaned back, his cinnamon roll finished, and sipped his coffee as he, too, watched the woman and children on the beach below them.

"It is. I love it here." She hadn't realized how much she missed the island. Missed living here. The island felt like... home.

Mason set down his mug and sighed. "I really should go find Dad and get to work."

"I'll go find Lillian."

And their quiet morning together ended with the unasked and unanswered question hanging between them. Was this the last morning they'd have like this?

~

"I WANT to run over and check on Etta this morning." Lillian put her coffee cup in the sink at The Nest.

"How about I get things going on taking down the hurricane shutters and setting things back in order?" Gary gave her a quick kiss on the cheek.

"I won't be long. I just worry about her after her fall. I think I'll take some food over to her, too. That way she can stay off her feet a bit more."

"That sounds like a good idea."

Lillian headed to the kitchen and found Jay already there, cooking. That didn't surprise her. Once she'd found out the electricity was back on, she knew he'd be here cooking and baking.

"Morning, Jay. Good to see you back here where you belong."

He turned and grinned. "Cinnamon rolls over there. And I made up some more sandwiches to feed whoever is hungry. Got more bread baking now, too."

"I'm going to take a basket of food over to Etta."

"Here I'll make you one. You sit and have a cup of coffee."

One more cup wouldn't hurt her, right? She

settled on a stool with her coffee and Jay rustled around, filling up a basket overflowing with food.

Robin came into the kitchen. "Computers are up, but the internet is down."

"Might take a while for it to come back."

"I already had a few phone calls about reservations."

"Let's see what all gets done today, and see about the bridge. If it's going to be ferry service only for a while we'll have to tell our guests to expect that. Then we'll make a decision on reopening." Lillian stood and took the basket from Jay. "Thanks for this. I won't be long. Gary is starting on taking down the shutters."

"I'll be out to help him as soon as this last batch of bread is done."

She hurried out of the kitchen and out into the sunshine, walking over to Etta's. People were busy in their yards clearing up the mess. A business on Main Street was tarping over a window that must have gotten broken. She hurried down the street until she got to Etta's.

She knocked on the door and called through the screened door. "It's Lillian."

"Come in," Etta called from inside.

She went in and found Etta sitting on the

couch with her leg propped up. Lillian held up the basket.

"I come bearing gifts. Lots of food from Jay."

"That was so sweet. Dr. Harden told me to try and stay off my leg as much as possible for a few days. I really want to get to the historical society and see how it fared. And clean up the mess I made when the bookcase crashed."

"You need to let us help you. Don't go there alone. Promise me, you'll call when you're ready to go, and we'll go with you."

"I don't want to be a bother."

"It's no bother. None at all." Lillian set the basket on the table beside Etta. "Is there anything you need? Anything at all?"

"No, I'm fine. Now that the electricity is on, I'm good. I'll be glad when the cell service quits cutting out."

"Hopefully it will be back to normal soon. We'll keep dropping in on you until it does."

"You don't need to. I'm sure I'll be fine."

Lillian shook her head. "Like you were fine at the historical society when that bookcase fell? Just let me do this. I'll feel better."

Etta threw up her hands and laughed. "Okay, you win. And I really do appreciate it."

"Okay, I'm heading back to the inn. You got your phone near you in case the cell service comes back?"

"I do."

"Okay, I'll check on you later." Lillian hurried outside, glad that Etta was doing okay. She worried about her living alone like that. Especially after her incident during the storm. But she also didn't want to hover and make Etta feel like she wasn't capable.

When Sara had hovered over her after her fall earlier this year, it had made Lillian a bit crazy. She wasn't an old lady and didn't want to be treated like one. She figured Etta felt the same way. Age was just a number... and she never planned on being ruled or defined by it.

CHAPTER 21

Zoe found Sara hauling the beach chairs from the lower storage area back to the beach area. "Sara, let me help you."

Sara paused and set down a chair. "That would be great. I told Aunt Lillian I'd haul these back out."

They made multiple trips, back and forth, until she thought she'd never be able to take another step. Who knew providing beach chairs at the inn was so much work?

Sara sank onto a chair. "I need a break."

Zoe plopped down on a chair next to her. "Thank goodness. I was wearing out."

"These storms are a lot of work, aren't they?"

"I know. All this work to prepare, then all

this work to put everything back like it was." She reached down and scooped up a handful of sand and let it sift through her fingers.

"Noah's house came through okay. Just a bit of damage to one corner of the roof."

"So, it's still Noah's house, huh? When are you going to start thinking of it as your house, too?" Zoe teased.

Sara laughed. "I should. It's just a hard habit to break. It's not like Noah hasn't said I can change anything and make it more mine."

"I'm sure it's hard to adjust to living with someone and moving into a place that was his."

"I actually thought it would be harder than it was. Noah is... well, he's the best."

"I'll agree with you on that." She scooped up another handful of sand.

"So, are you going to move back to the house? You don't have to stay at the inn, you know."

"I know."

Sara stared at her and a small smile played at the corners of her lips. "But you like staying here while Mason is here, don't you?"

She let out a long breath. "I... do."

"So, you like him?"

She turned and looked out at the water,

trying to find the right words. "I do care about him. It's silly. I haven't known him that long. But I feel like I really *know* him." She shrugged. "That he knows me. That he really *sees* me. How can that happen so quickly?"

Sara shook her head. "I don't know. Sometimes your heart just has its own timeline."

"I guess."

"Have you told him how you feel?"

Zoe leaned back on the chair. "No, of course not. I mean... it's so soon. And he's leaving to go home. And... well, it would be better if I just keep quiet and not complicate things."

"I think it's always better to tell the truth. Who knows? Maybe he feels the same way."

"I don't know..."

"At least think about it." Sara got up. "I should get back to work."

She stood. "I'm coming." She gave one last longing glance at the chair and followed Sara back to the storage room.

Mason looked up from where he was bundling fallen palm branches to drag them to the street to be picked up later by the town. Zoe came walking across the grassy area, a smile on her face.

His breath caught at the sight of her. Her hair whipped around in the breeze that had picked up and she caught it with one hand as she crossed the distance. One delicate hand, with those long fingers of hers that he loved to lace with his own.

How had he let her get under his skin so quickly? She walked up to him and he grabbed her hand, glancing around briefly. When he didn't see anyone, he kissed her quickly, though he wanted to linger there. Kiss her again. And maybe again. But he resisted. Kind of. One more quick kiss.

"Well, that's a nice hello." Her mouth played in a smile and her eyes sparkled.

And her eyes. He could get lost in those eyes.

And when had he become some kind of romantic fool?

"Let me help you," she offered.

"You don't need to. You could just sit and keep me company."

"No, I want to help. I'll go get those

branches over there." She pointed to a tree a short distance away.

He knew better than to argue with her, so he nodded. He watched her walk away, her long, tanned legs stretching out with each stride. A gust of wind tossed her hair again, and she grabbed at it, holding it in one hand. She leaned over to pick up a palm branch and he watched her every move.

He really should get back to work, but he couldn't resist watching her. Staring at her, really. A funny flip of his heart didn't help things. She wove some kind of spell over him.

He leaned down to pick up a branch at his feet, and as he straightened, his heart started pounding. Was that tree... falling? Headed right in Zoe's direction? "Zoe, watch out."

He dropped the branch and sprinted toward her, watching in shock as a nearby palm tree began to tilt next to her. "The tree," he shouted as loudly as he could, waving his arms to get her attention.

She turned to glance at him and then whirled back around, seeing the tree, her arms raised above her.

Her scream tore at his very soul.

"Zoe."

He raced the final steps. "Zoe." He dug through the palm fronds, clearing them away until he saw her face. "Zoe." She lay there, her eyes closed, blood across her forehead.

She opened her eyes. "Well, that was... scary."

"Are you okay?" She wasn't. There was blood.

"I think so."

He dug around in the foliage, moving back branches. The main trunk had barely missed crushing her. She was just covered with the top branches. At least she hadn't been crushed. He thought he might faint then as the relief swelled through him. Some hero he was. All he could think was he could have lost her.

"Let me get you out of there." He bent back branches and tore at them, clearing the way.

She reached out a hand and he took it in his. Firmly. He didn't ever want to let her go. She scrambled to her feet and landed against him. He wrapped her in his arms and held her tightly.

He could hear voices calling in the distance, but he ignored them. Ignored everything but this woman in his arms. He pulled back slightly and gently swept her hair away from her face. "Are you okay?"

"I am. I think I am. It just... wow." She gave him a weak smile.

His father came racing up to him. "I looked out and saw the tree down. Saw Mason digging through it. Are you okay?" His dad frowned. "No, you're not. You're bleeding."

"I am?" Zoe looked down at the blood on her shirt.

"We need to get you checked out." Mason carefully looked her over. "It's here. There's a gash on your arm."

Zoe looked at her arm. "Well, there is."

"Come on, let's take her inside." His dad motioned toward the inn.

Mason wrapped an arm firmly around Zoe's waist and they slowly made their way inside. With each step, he told himself to calm down. That she was okay. But he couldn't help but notice the tremble in his hands as he carefully supported her along the walkway.

CHAPTER 22

Zoe thought she might scream if everyone didn't stop hovering over her. She knew they meant well, but she was okay. Really. As she kept telling them.

She looked up to see Noah rushing in through the main door.

"Zoe, Lil called. Are you okay?" Her uncle raced over and sank to his knees in front of her.

"I'm fine." See, she would just keep repeating it until someone believed her.

"What's that?" He eyed the bandage on her arm.

"It's just a little cut."

"It's not so little," Lillian contradicted her. "But I cleaned it up and bandaged it for her."

"Does she need to see Dr. Harden?" Noah's brow creased.

"No. I don't," Zoe insisted.

"Lillian said a tree fell on you?" Noah scanned her slowly, carefully.

"It mostly missed me." She shrugged.

"Well, I've come to take you home."

"Nah, all my stuff is here. I'm fine." Her voice was a tad bit shakier than she'd like.

"I'll collect your things. Or you can come back later and get them. You're coming home with me." Noah's voice didn't hold any room for argument.

But she didn't want to leave. She looked over at Mason who gave her a nod. What did that nod mean? That he wanted her to stay? That she should leave with Noah?

"I'll get her things and bring them over. How about that?" Mason offered.

Ah, he was fine with her leaving. Okay, then. Perfect. That's fine. Really it was. He didn't care if she left... on what might be their last day together.

Noah reached out and helped her up. "That would be great. Thanks." He turned to Lillian. "And thank you so much for getting her all bandaged up."

She stood by herself, annoyed that she still felt a bit shaky. "I'm fine," she lied to herself as well as everyone else. She gritted her teeth. She *was* fine. Just a bit battered and bruised. And a bit tired. It wasn't every day she had a tree fall on her.

"I'll help you out." Mason stepped forward, concern coloring his eyes.

"I've got her," Noah said brusquely as he took her uninjured arm.

She gave Mason a smile that she hoped said she was *fine* and leaned against Noah—just a tiny bit—as they walked out of the inn.

MASON PACKED up Zoe's things, carefully folding the clothes she'd tossed randomly on a chair. He smiled as he did it. The woman just didn't grasp the concept of orderly whereas he was methodical and organized to a fault. But it was just one more thing that he found adorable about her.

Gathering up the things she'd left in the bathroom—scattered all over the counter—he walked out and glanced around the bedroom, making sure he'd gotten everything. With one last look, he went back to the main room of the suite.

The emptiness of the space stifled him. He missed seeing Zoe here. Her laugh, her smile, her teasing. Even her mess. But it was better she was back with her uncle. It had been plain to see how worried Noah was about her, and he didn't blame him. He'd been so worried about Zoe, too. When that tree had started to fall and he'd seen Zoe standing there... his heart had just about stopped.

He shook the thoughts away.

He'd really, *really* wanted to ask her to stay here at the suite. Just one more night. But that would have been selfish. She'd had quite an ordeal and needed her family. He stepped out of the suite and closed the door firmly behind him.

He got downstairs with Zoe's things and ran into his dad.

"Get everything?"

"I hope so. I'm going to head over to Zoe's and give them to her."

His dad nodded. "Then what?"

"Then I need to head back to Seattle. I've already called the pilot. I leave in the morning. I've been away too long. I really need to get back."

His dad frowned, chewed his lip, then let out a long sigh. "Things are pretty much under control here. I'm coming with you, son. Need to talk to the Board of Directors."

And what would his father be telling the board? Was he coming back to run the company? Or was he going to stay here on the island? His father's face didn't give him a clue, but he figured his dad would tell him when the time was right.

He nodded. "Okay, sounds good."

After driving over to Noah's house, he parked in front of it and sat in the car for a few minutes, steeling himself. Readying himself to say goodbye to Zoe. And this time, he meant it. He wasn't going to be turning around at the airport and heading right back. He'd run out of excuses. And he had responsibilities to the company. It was time.

He climbed out of the car and trudged up to the front door. Noah opened it and let him in. "She's tired. She needs some rest. I don't think you should stay long."

Mason nodded.

"She's in the back sunroom." Noah pointed through the main room.

Mason walked slowly across the space, each

step dragging him down. Smothering him. But he put on a cheerful—if fake—smile when he entered the sunroom. "Hey there."

Zoe looked up at him and smiled. *That* smile. The one that took his breath away and drove him a bit crazy. And he wanted to kiss those lips, but he was well aware that Noah was just steps away, hovering near.

"I brought your things." He set her belongings on a chair.

"That was nice of you."

"I hope I got everything."

"If not, I'll go back and get anything you missed."

Simple conversation, if a bit inane, as he stalled, unwilling to tell her what he'd really come to say.

She looked up at him and her brow wrinkled. And he sensed the exact moment that she knew already.

"You're leaving, aren't you?" Her eyes held a cloak of sadness.

"I am. I need to get back to Seattle. Dad's going with me. We're leaving first thing in the morning."

She nodded slightly. "Well, your job is there. I knew you'd have to leave soon."

She scooted up on the couch and he sat down beside her. "I'm going to miss you, Zoe."

"I'll miss you too. These couple of weeks... they've been..." She looked down at her hands, not finishing her sentence.

He glanced out of the sunroom, not seeing Noah, and took her hand in his. "These weeks have been wonderful. I really enjoyed spending time with you. I wish..." He looked directly into her eyes. "I wish things were different."

"But they aren't." Her voice was low.

"No, they aren't."

"Do you think you'll come back to visit... visit the island?"

"Probably. I'm not sure how often I can get away, though." He gave her a weak smile. "But I'm just a mere six-hour flight away from here."

Noah came walking into the room and Mason dropped Zoe's hand. "Here, Zoe, I brought you some tea." He set the teacup on the coffee table. "You should rest."

Mason took his clue. "I should go then." He stood.

"Uncle Noah, can you give us a minute?"

Noah nodded and left the sunroom, though Mason could hear him rustling around in the adjoining room.

"You take care of yourself, Zoe Birch."

She nodded.

He leaned down and kissed the side of her cheek, turned, and walked out of the room, knowing that if he kissed her lips, if he said anything more, that he'd never be able to make himself leave.

Zoe watched Mason leave and reached a hand up to touch her cheek where he'd kissed her. Then she touched her lips. The lips she'd hoped he'd kiss just one more time.

A lone tear trailed down her cheek and she did nothing to wipe it away. Its hot path down her cheek just reminded her of what she already was missing. And he hadn't even left the island yet.

Noah poked his head in. "You okay?"

"I will be." She reached for the tea and tried to put on a more cheerful expression. *She was fine.*

"So, he's leaving?"

"He is. Has to get back to Seattle."

Noah crossed over to her. "I... I was afraid

you were going to get hurt. You've fallen for him. Haven't you?"

She looked into the teacup, then back at her uncle. "A bit."

Noah scowled. "He should have left you alone instead of hanging around you every minute he was in town. He knew he was leaving."

"Noah, I love you for caring, but just... I enjoyed spending time with him. I had fun. It was an incredible few weeks."

"I just hate seeing you hurt."

"I'll be fine. Don't worry about me."

Noah snorted a laugh. "As if that will ever happen." He turned to leave. "I'll let you rest. Call out if you need me."

She settled back on the couch, sipping the tea and trying to imagine what her life would be like now that Mason was gone.

And she didn't really like the picture she saw. But there was nothing she could do about it. It was life. Life threw curves and the best a person could do was learn to adapt to them.

CHAPTER 23

Lillian watched Gary pack early the next morning. He'd put on dress slacks and a button-down long-sleeve shirt. He'd tucked a tie in his carry on. So different than the shorts, t-shirts, and sandals she was used to seeing. This was Gary the business owner. Gary the CEO.

"You sure you're going to be okay here? You've got the re-opening under control?" His forehead creased with worry.

"I do. And Jay and Robin will help with what's left. I'll be fine."

"I still feel bad leaving you to deal with the rest of it." He straightened and looked at her. "But I've left this hanging long enough. And since Mason has the jet heading back today, it seemed like now was a good time."

"You're going to tell them you're coming back as CEO, aren't you?" She got up and rested her hand on his arm.

He took her in his arms. "I'm still not certain. I need to talk to Mason and sort it all out."

"I'm fine with whatever you decide. We'll work it out. If you need to be there some of the time, we'll figure it out."

"I don't know what I did to deserve you, Lil."

She reached up and touched his face. "I'm the lucky one. Lucky to have found you. We both had our own lives before we found each other. We'll figure out a way to make this new life work."

He kissed her gently, then turned to close his suitcase. "I'll call when I get there. And probably way too many times. Enough that you'll get sick of me calling."

She laughed. "I doubt that."

She walked with him out to the lobby where Mason was waiting for them.

"Ready, Dad?"

"I am."

"Lillian, you take care," Mason said as he grabbed his suitcase.

The front door of the inn swung open and in breezed Camille with Delbert Hamilton in her wake. "Lillian. Good. There you are. Could Delbert and I have your best suite?"

"We're not quite opened yet, Camille." Camille Montgomery was the last thing she needed right now.

"But Mama's house doesn't have electricity and I just can't abide by staying there another night. There's no air-conditioning. And our cook can't come to make us any food." Camille looked truly distressed. "You *have* to let us stay here." Camille stopped just short of stomping her foot like a two-year-old throwing a tantrum. *Just* short.

Lillian sighed. "Okay, as long as you know we're not fully functional yet. Jay has been putting out sandwiches for meals. We weren't planning on opening for a few more days. There's still some cleanup to do."

Delbert walked over and took her hand. "Anything's fine, Lillian. Really. We're very appreciative of it, right Camille?" He looked over at Camille.

She just flipped her hair on her shoulder. "Well, it is an inn, right? A place where people can stay? I don't know why she wouldn't want us here." Camille turned to Lillian. "And you do have a decent suite, don't you? We'll need two bedrooms, of course. But it must be a *nice* suite."

Lillian clenched her teeth, rolled her shoulders a bit, then forced a smile. "Yes, of course. The rooms are cleaned, but not quite ready. I'll get a room made up for you."

"Nonsense. We'll make it up ourselves. You have enough to do getting the inn ready. You point me to clean towels and sheets and I'll have that suite ready to go in no time," Delbert insisted.

"Delbert, really. You're going to clean the room and make the beds? Have you ever even *done* that?"

Delbert laughed. "Of course, darling. I told you I started at the bottom with Hamilton hotels. My father made sure of that. I'd venture to say I've done about every job a hotel has at one point in time or the other."

Lillian turned back to Gary. "I better get them settled in."

Gary wrapped an arm around her and gave her a quick kiss. He whispered in her ear. "I'll miss you. Oh, and good luck with Camille." He winked at her as he pulled away.

A sudden wave of loneliness swept through her as Gary and Mason left. *Oh, that was ridiculous.* She'd be busy. She had the inn to run. She turned back to Delbert and Camille.

"Okay, let's get you all settled in your room."

"Do you have someone to take our bags up?" Camille frowned.

"Nope."

"I've got them, darlin'. Lillian is already doing us a favor letting us stay here before she's quite ready to open."

Camille let out a long-suffering sigh. "Well, we *are* paying guests."

Lillian turned her back on Camille and headed to the reception desk to get the key. Maybe Camille would spend all her time in her room. One could only hope...

LILLIAN FOUND Jay and Robin in the kitchen after she got Delbert and Camille settled into their suite. True to his word, Delbert had taken the sheets and towels and insisted they'd be fine.

"So, we have guests."

"I thought we weren't opening for a few more days?" Robin raised an eyebrow.

"We weren't. But Camille and Delbert needed a place to stay and... well... I let them stay." She couldn't help the long sigh that escaped.

"Delbert will be fine." Jay shrugged. "But Camille is always a handful. Hope she doesn't expect my normal meals. I still need to get more supplies before we open fully. Going to try and take the ferry to the mainland and load up."

"She'll have to take whatever we have."

"So, Robin and I were just going to check out the camera in your office." Jay pulled out his phone. "I think I have it working again after the storm."

He tapped on his phone, looked at it, then frowned. "Hey, there's some video it captured. Must have been right before the storm. It syncs up to a recording in the cloud, so we can see it."

He tapped some more buttons and she and Robin crowded around him, looking at his phone.

"I need to make that bigger. Is that..."

"That's Dana, isn't it? Arguing with someone in my office?"

Jay enlarged the photo. "It is. The date and time stamp say it's the day we closed up the inn." He turned to Robin. "Remember when we saw her coming back out of the kitchen after we closed up Magnolia House?"

"I do." Robin frowned. "But Dana? You think *she* stole from Lillian?"

Jay stared at the photo on the phone and frowned. "I know this guy."

"You do?" Lillian looked at him.

"He used to do maintenance and repairs at that restaurant. You know, the one I was fired from and they accused me of stealing their money."

"That cannot be a coincidence," Robin said.

"No, it can't. And Dana must know him." Lillian frowned. "It looks like they're fighting or arguing."

"We're going to have to find Dana." Jay stared at the phone screen again. "I can't believe it. This guy must have been the one who stole from the other place, too."

"Possibly. Well, probably." Lillian sighed. "We'll deal with Dana when she comes back. Send her to me when she comes in."

"I'll be coming with her. You're not dealing with this alone," Jay insisted.

"That's probably best." She turned to go. "I'm headed to my office. Let me know if she comes in."

CHAPTER 24

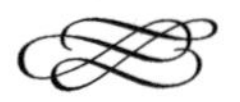

"I can't believe that Dana is part of this." Robin turned to him after Lillian left.

"I can't either."

"She seems so responsible. And she's a sweet girl." Robin frowned. "Or at least I thought she was."

"She had us all fooled." Jay set down the pot he was holding with more force than he meant to. "I'm usually a good judge of character, and she struck me as honest and—" He scowled, annoyed at himself, upset that he'd missed any signs of Dana's deception. "Doesn't matter. We have her on video."

He paused and frowned at the sound of voices outside the kitchen door. He strode over to the doorway. There, standing right outside the door was Dana and a man. The man had his back to the doorway and a firm grip on each of Dana's shoulders, shaking her. "You will do as you're told," the man snarled.

"Dad, you're hurting me."

Dad? This man was Dana's father?

"Then do as you're told. Give me back the money."

"I'm going to return it. You can't steal from Miss Lillian. You can't."

Jay tried to process what was happening right in front of him. As he paused the man raised a hand ready to strike Dana.

Jay jumped forward and grabbed the man's hand and the man whirled around, losing his grip on Dana.

"Ah, the infamous thief." The man's lips twisted into a mocking grin. "How'd that go for you at your last job? They were mighty quick to convict you."

There he was. The man on the video with Dana. The man he thought he recognized, and now he was sure of it. The man who'd stolen from his last job and made it so Jay had ended up in jail. He watched the man closely, watching his every move, still clasping the man's hand in his.

"And yet, it was you who stole from them," Jay finally said.

"Haven't met a safe yet that I can't crack," the man bragged, then jerked his hand away from Jay.

"Dana, step away from him." Jay motioned to the side with his head.

She took a few steps back, out of the man's reach.

"This is your father?"

Dana nodded, her eyes wide.

"You can call me Freddy, though." The man tossed another mean grin.

He kept looking between Dana and her father. "And you helped him steal from Lillian?"

"I— I didn't want to. But he—"

"Shut your mouth, girl," the man snarled again.

Dana took a few more steps back.

He felt Robin come up to stand beside him. "What's going on?"

"I'm sorry, Robin. So sorry. I was bringing back the money. I was." Tears trailed down Dana's face.

Robin took a step forward. "Dana—"

"No, stop." Jay held out a hand. "We're

just going to call the sheriff and get this cleared up." He reached into his pocket for his phone.

That distraction was a mistake. Before he could comprehend what was happening, the man grabbed Robin and pulled her tight against him.

"No, you're not."

Jay couldn't mistake the glint of a knife in the man's hand. He swallowed, willing himself to stay calm and think. Just think.

"Dad, let her go. Don't hurt her," Dana pleaded.

"I think this little lady is my ticket out of here. Give your phone to my daughter."

Jay nodded and took a step toward Dana. He reached out his phone to her without letting his gaze leave Robin and felt the phone taken out from his grip.

"Okay, there. Dana has the phone. Now let Robin go." He took a step toward the man.

"I think she'll just take a little boat ride with me. Until I get safely off this island." Freddy's eyes narrowed.

"Dad, let her go. I have his phone. You have time. Just go."

"I think I need this bit of insurance. I'll have this little lady call you to come get her someplace on the mainland. After I'm long gone."

"You're not taking her anywhere." Jay's words came out forcefully. He honestly was surprised he could speak over the pounding of his heart and the racing of his pulse. He could see the fright in Robin's eyes, and there was no way this man was taking her anywhere. Not if he could help it.

"Ah, but I am." There was no mistaking the assured, threatening tone.

"Jay..." Robin looked at him, then she looked down and a little behind him.

In an instant, he knew what she was saying to him. Saying without any words. He nodded slightly.

Before Freddy knew what was happening, Robin slammed her foot down onto his, elbowed him in the gut, then threw her weight forward. Freddy lost his grip with one of his arms, and she wrenched further away.

Jay swooped down and scooped up the brick they used to prop the door open and swung it at the man, catching his shoulder. Freddy yelled and lost his grip on Robin. Jay wrapped his arm around Robin, whirling around, catching her as they both tumbled to the ground. Robin sagged against him.

"I'll get even. Don't think I won't." Freddy raced off.

Dana rushed over. "Are you okay? I'm so sorry. So very sorry."

"Are you okay?" Jay looked at Robin carefully, scanning, looking for any sign of harm.

"Just rattled."

She clung to him and he held her tight, stroking her hair. "You're safe now."

Dana reached out to hand him his phone. "Here, call the police. Maybe they can stop him."

Jay took the phone with one hand but kept his other arm firmly around Robin. "You okay to stand?"

Robin nodded and he helped her to her feet.

"The police will want to arrest me too..." Dana wiped away the tears from her face.

Robin walked over to Dana, and to his surprise, Robin reached out and touched Dana's face, brushing back the girl's hair.

"He hit you, didn't he?" Robin asked.

"He— sometimes. A lot. I couldn't do anything right."

Robin pushed up the sleeve on Dana's shirt and looked down. "Jay, look at this."

He walked over and saw the bruise on Dana's arm and the one on her face that she had tried to carefully cover with makeup. The tears had washed away her subterfuge.

"What's going on here?"

He turned at the sound of Lillian's voice.

"Oh, Lillian. I'm so sorry. I tried to return the money, but he caught me." Dana rushed out her words in big, body-wracking sobs.

"Who caught you?" Lillian frowned, looking at him, then Robin, then Dana.

"It's a long story, Lillian. Let's go inside and decide what to do next." He led them back into the kitchen and they sat at a small table while he explained what happened.

"You're okay, Robin?" Lillian's face was creased with worry.

"I'm okay."

"If we call the sheriff, he'll know you lied about finding the money before. But if we don't call, the guy gets away."

"We're calling Sheriff Dave. I'll explain everything. The man needs to be stopped. And he needs to be stopped from hurting Dana anymore." Lillian reached out and took Dana's hand.

"And they'll want to arrest me for the part I played in everything." Tears rolled down Dana's face again.

"We'll see if we can sort that out, too." Lillian stood. "Dana, come with me. I'm going to go make that call. Jay, make some tea for Robin. Hot tea always helps soothe a rough time."

He got up to make the tea, glad to have something to keep him busy. Because what he really wanted to do was to chase after Freddy and teach him a lesson or two.

His hands shook as he put on the kettle, glancing back to assure himself that Robin was still sitting at the table, she was still okay. His hands curled into fists of anger, but he commanded himself to take some big, long breaths. He stretched out his long fingers and grabbed a cup for Robin's tea, surprised to see that his hands were *still* trembling.

He sensed, more than felt, Robin come up to stand behind him and wrap her arms around his waist. "I'm okay, Jay. Really I am."

He turned around in her embrace, kissing the top of her head and pulling her close. He ran his hands through her hair and stroked her back, all the while chanting silently to himself. *It's okay. It's all okay. Robin is fine.*

But was he?

ROBIN FINISHED UP HER TEA. Lillian was right, a good cup of tea did settle her down. Well, kind of. She was still a bit jittery. It had all happened so fast.

"You're staying with me tonight. I don't want you at the bungalow until Freddy is caught." Jay's eyes dissuaded any argument, but he softened the command. "Please? I won't sleep at all thinking about you at the bungalow."

She wasn't really looking forward to going back to the bungalow alone, either.

"And call Charlotte and tell her to stay at Ruby's until we find Freddy. I don't want her there and Freddy showing up looking for you."

Robin frowned. Jay was right. She didn't want to put Charlotte in danger. She stood and walked outside, staying close to the doorway, and called her friend. Charlotte listened to what happened and assured her that she'd stay with Ruby.

She walked back inside to find Lillian talking to Jay.

"I want Jay to take you home." Lillian turned to her.

"But you have Camille and Delbert here. Jay will need to at least make some food for them."

"Dana's going to make it."

"Really?" Robin tried to keep the surprise out of her voice.

"Yes. She's talking to the sheriff now, giving some ideas on where her father might be. I told the sheriff I won't be pressing charges against the girl." Lillian shrugged. "I think she was just doing what she had to do to survive in a bad situation. I'm giving her a room to stay in here at the inn for now. I don't want her going back to her place."

And somehow, Robin wasn't a bit surprised. This was classic Lillian. Giving someone a second chance. Taking care of someone when life had dealt them a tough road.

"Come on, Robs. Lillian has a good idea. I'll get you back to my place. Besides, we should check on Sunny and Barney, right?" Jay took her hand.

"So, you two run along." Lillian practically pushed them out the door. "And, Jay, you keep an eye on her until Freddy is found."

CHAPTER 25

The next morning Lillian went to the historical society along with Robin and Jay to help Etta clean things up. Etta hobbled around with her crutches though Lillian did her best to try to make her sit and keep her foot elevated. But Etta kept popping up to get one thing or another.

She sent Robin and Jay to the storage room to clean up the mess from the fallen bookcase while she and Etta unloaded some rubber containers Etta had filled in case there was damage from the storm.

Robin and Jay came back to the main room after an hour or so. "We've finished up in there. What are you two doing?" Robin crossed over to the table.

"I was telling Etta about Anna and her Johnny fella from the journal. Anna is listed as missing in the storm, and her journal ends right before the storm. Johnny's father was the lightkeeper on the island."

"And I had a listing of all the lightkeepers. I found Johnny's last name."

"That's some good detective work." Robin peered over their shoulders.

"We're looking up to see if we can find out anything about them." Lillian was already crushed that Anna went missing in the storm. She'd feel a bit better if she could at least have good news about Johnny. Like maybe he'd gone on to live a happy life. Or some thread of hope.

Etta paused and looked up, a sad expression crossing her face. "Oh, Lillian, look. Johnny is listed as missing in the storm, too."

"Oh, no." Her heart tightened and sadness swept through her. It was hard to explain. She didn't really know them and it was so many years ago. But still. It saddened her. She sighed. "I had hoped they'd end up together and get their happily-ever-after. Or that at least Johnny did."

Etta closed the folder of papers. "I guess not. I'm sorry, Lillian."

"That's that, I suppose. The end of the journal mystery. Though we still didn't find any descendants of Anna's family to return the journal to." Lillian stood, pushing aside the thought of the missing couple. Or trying to. She had work to do. "Well, enough of this. I have an inn to run. You'll take it easy if we leave you here? Promise?"

"I'll take it easy." Etta nodded.

"At least stay off ladders," Jay admonished her.

She grinned. "I will do that."

Lillian left with Robin and Jay, and yet she couldn't shake the sadness that lingered over finding out the news about first Anna, then Johnny. Starcrossed lovers who never had their chance at happiness.

CHAPTER 26

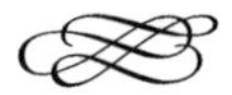

Uncle Noah was driving her nuts. No matter how many times she insisted she was okay, he hovered around. Always and constantly. But, being back on the island had made one thing clear to Zoe. She'd thought she had to move away to make it on her own, prove herself. But now... all she wanted was to move back home.

Well, not in the same house as Sara and Noah. It was way too cramped for all of them. But back to the island. Find a job here. She'd even turned in her notice at her job.

Noah came walking into the sunroom. "Do you need anything?"

"Aren't you supposed to be working at the

community center?" She eyed him over the rim of her glass of sweet tea.

"I was, but I just stopped in to check on you."

"Uncle Noah. I. Am. Fine." She didn't know how to make it any clearer to him.

He sank onto the couch beside her. "I know you are. I do. It's just... it's my responsibility to keep you safe. To take care of you."

"No, it's my own responsibility to take care of myself. Make my own decisions." She eyed him. "And, by the way, I've made a big decision."

He cocked his head to the side and she could see him bracing himself.

"I'm moving back to the island."

His eyes flew open wide. "You're what?"

"Moving back here. But—" She held up a hand. "I'm not living here with you and Sara. I'm finding my own place. I've talked with Lisa and I'm going to move in with her."

"The two best friends together again." A wide smile overtook Noah's features. "This is great news. Great."

"I've missed living here. I love the island. The people here."

Noah took her hand. "I'd love to have you back here."

"Then it's settled. And Lisa has a couple leads for me on a job."

"You'll find one." He hugged her. "This is the best news ever."

And it was good news. She was sure of her decision. And she *was* happy. Except… she missed Mason. He was the missing link to everything being perfect living back on the island.

CHAPTER 27

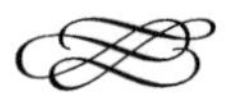

Mason sat at the conference table with his father, going over notes on what they were going to say at the scheduled meeting of the upper management of the company.

His dad was going through a stack of papers that had accumulated while he'd been gone. He frowned when he picked up one with a handwritten address on it. He sliced it open and read it. "Well."

"Well, what?"

"It's from Brian."

"The guy that practically brought you to ruin?"

"It's about time I tell you the whole story. I found him. He was on an island. With his wife and daughter."

"I didn't know he was married."

"It's a long story, but he stole the money from the company to pay for some medical procedures for his daughter. She was dying. Anyway, he promised me he'd come back and turn himself in after she had one more surgery."

"And?"

"And he's back and scheduled to be arraigned this week."

"I haven't heard any news of it." Mason frowned.

"I'm sure once the press gets ahold of it, it will be all over the news." His father pushed a piece of paper across the table toward him. "And he still had stock in the company and turned it over to me. Looks like you and I have controlling interest again."

Mason frowned. "So he did it—stole the money—for his daughter?"

"Yes, and it didn't make it right, but honestly, I'd do anything for you too, son."

Mason looked at him for a moment. "Even come back as CEO for the company?"

"Why, do you want to step down?"

"I— I didn't plan on having this position. Not for years anyway."

"But you're doing a fine job with it."

Mason leaned back in his chair, choosing his words carefully. "You know how you and mom were? Working all the time? It consumed your lives."

"I know it did. And I'm sorry about that. We weren't the best parents." His dad leaned forward. "Is this about Zoe?"

"No. Well, kind of." He raked his hand through his hair. "I just... I was caught off guard. I wasn't looking for... anything. But then... I found Zoe. And I care about her. When that tree was falling and I thought for a second that I'd lose her... I couldn't breathe. Couldn't move."

"Have you told her how you feel?"

"No." He looked down at the stack of papers before him and let out a long sigh. "No, I didn't tell her. And besides, I have responsibilities here. She has a job there. Well, not on the island, but all the way across the country from here."

His father studied his face for a long while, then reached out and touched his hand. "You know, son. Sometimes you need to do what you want to do instead of what you think you're expected to do."

He looked at his father and felt his face break into a wry grin. "You know, Dad, you could take your own advice."

His dad's eyes twinkled, and a slow smile spread across his face. "About that. I have an idea."

CHAPTER 28

Betty sat out on the front porch of the retirement center. She'd been sitting outside for about half an hour. Jay had called to say that he and Robin were bringing Barney for a visit when they came over on the ferry to pick up some supplies for the inn. She couldn't wait to see Barney. She'd missed him so much.

And she knew Barney hated storms. She hoped he'd handled the hurricane okay.

She pushed to her feet when she saw them pull up in the parking lot and waved her hand, a smile sweeping across her face when Jay got out of the car with Barney in tow.

Barney barked and wagged his tail, tugging Jay across the lot and up the stairs. She collapsed back into her chair and leaned down to wrap the dog in a hug. "Oh, Barney. You made it through the storm. It was a bad one, wasn't it? I bet you weren't very happy."

"He doesn't like storms much, does he?" Robin asked.

"Not at all. But he did okay?"

"He was fine," Jay answered.

But she didn't miss the looks that passed between Robin and Jay. Who knew what mischief Barney had gotten into. She petted him again. "Now, Barney, you need to be good for Jay." Barney wagged his tail.

"Here, come sit down. I got us some lemonade." She motioned to the tray with a big pitcher of lemonade and three glasses.

Robin poured them all drinks and settled beside her while Jay lounged against the porch railing. Barney sat right at her feet. She'd missed that. She petted him again and heard the resounding thump of his tail on the wooden porch.

"I heard the bridge was out during the storm." She shook her head. "I didn't know if you'd be able to come over here this soon."

"We took the ferry. But they've inspected the bridge. It wasn't as bad as they feared. I think the bridge will be open before long. But for now, the ferry runs regularly and a few tugs are bringing over flat barges of supplies." Jay took a sip of lemonade.

"But the town did okay? Not much damage?"

"We were really lucky with this storm," Robin said.

"I was worried about all of you. I'm so glad you're okay." She reached down to pet her dog. "And Barney is adjusting?"

"He's doing fine," Jay assured her.

"I'm sure he misses you, but he's quite taken with Jay," Robin added.

"I'm so grateful you could take him."

"I was glad to. I'm glad for his company."

"Oh, did you know that George and Ida live here? They were talking about a journal Lillian found in their old home, Magnolia House. Some kind of mystery surrounding it while Lillian tried to figure out who wrote it?"

Robin paused the slow rocking of her chair. "Well, that's kind of sad. Lillian has found out more. The journal was written by an Anna Smith. And she had a secret boyfriend, Johnny. His dad was the lightkeeper."

Betty frowned. "The lightkeeper?" A slow

recollection flowed through her. Anna Smith. Hadn't heard that name in a very long time.

"But it looks like both Anna and Johnny were listed as missing in a big hurricane that came through the town. Lillian is kind of sad about it. She was hoping that Anna and Johnny found their happily ever after. But Anna died."

Betty broke into a wide grin. "Oh, no she didn't. Do I have good news for Lillian."

"What?" Jay frowned and looked at her.

"I know you've done so much already, but do you think you could take me to the island so I can see Lillian?"

"Of course. You can visit her and then we'll bring you back." Robin stood. "And I can't wait to hear your story."

"Well, let's wait until I can tell Lillian."

Lillian looked up from the reception desk to see Robin, Jay, and Betty Gleason standing before her. All three looked like they held the answer to some big secret.

"Betty, what are you doing here? It's so good to see you." She came around the counter.

"I have some news for you. News I wanted to deliver in person."

What news could Betty possibly have? Intrigued, Lillian led the way over to a sitting area in the lobby. They all settled and she turned to Betty, waiting.

"Well, I heard about the journal you found."

A ping tugged at Lillian's heart. "Yes, Anna Smith's journal. It's sad though. She and her beau died in a hurricane."

"No... they didn't."

Lillian leaned forward, searching Betty's face. "What?"

"They didn't die. They married."

"But how? They were listed as missing..."

"They were listed, but really they'd eloped. They didn't know everyone thought they were missing in the storm. They'd left a letter, but that did go missing in the storm."

"I don't understand..."

"They stayed away for a couple of years because Anna's father was not a fan of Johnny's. But then they had a child and came back to see if they could work things out. Her father took one look at that little baby girl, and, well. The rest of the family lore had it that that little girl could do no wrong and brought the family back together. He spoiled that little girl and the whole family got their happily-ever-after."

"How do you know all this?"

"Anna was my great grandmother on my mother's side of the family."

Happiness rushed through Lillian. Anna and Johnny had found each other. They married. It was the perfect ending for the journal story. Lillian jumped up. "I'll be right back."

She hurried to The Nest and back to the lobby and handed the journal to Betty. "Here you go. Here's the journal."

Betty clutched it tightly to her chest. "Oh, a bit of my family history. This is wonderful."

"And one more thing." Lillian held out the piece of turquoise sea glass. "We found this with the journal."

"Oh, it's beautiful." Betty set the journal down and took the sea glass, turning it over and over in her hand.

"You should make it into a pretty necklace or something," Robin suggested.

"That's a great idea, dear. It's so pretty."

Lillian sat back, content that she'd found the end of Anna's and Johnny's story, and that their story had finished with such a remarkable, happy ending.

CHAPTER 29

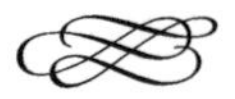

Robin popped into her bungalow with Barney the next day. She really needed to get a few more outfits if she was going to stay with Jay much longer. Though, maybe she should just move into the inn for a bit. She did worry about what the town gossiped about, even though she had her own room at Jay's.

She shook her head. She should listen to Lillian and ignore the town gossip. It made Jay feel better to have her near while Freddy was still missing. Though hopefully, by now, he was miles away from Belle Island.

And Barney and Sunny were getting along great at Jay's house. She swore the kitten got bigger every day. She should just let things go along like they were for now. But she *did* need those clothes.

She unlocked the door and she and Barney went inside. "Barney, I won't be long. Just need to get a few things."

She checked through her mail, then headed to the bedroom to pack a small bag with a few more outfits. And shoes. She needed more shoes. She hummed under her breath as she packed. Life was pretty good these days. She and Jay were a couple. The inn had opened back up. And soon the bridge would be open, too. Though the ferry was doing a great job of hauling the tourists and day visitors to the island and business was picking up for the town.

She walked back into the front room, lost in her thoughts of her perfect little world, and froze.

Freddy stood in the doorway.

She took a step back. "What do you want?"

"To get off this blasted island. I need a boat."

"I don't have one."

"But your friend Charlotte can get us one." He took a menacing step toward her.

"She—she doesn't have a boat."

"But her boyfriend does. I hear all about

things on the island from Dana. Been living here with her for months now."

Too bad for Dana. She was so much better off now without him.

She looked to her right and left but didn't see anything she could grab to protect herself, and she wasn't into the whole grab her and hold a knife to her thing again. She sensed, more than saw, Barney come up to her side and growl at Freddy.

"Keep the dog away. I mean it." Freddy swung his arm wide and she couldn't miss the glint of a knife.

"Barney, it's okay." She lied to the dog who stayed stubbornly at her side.

"So, you call your Charlotte buddy and get a boat."

"What will I tell her? She knows I don't boat."

"Think fast, kiddo. 'Cause I need one to get off the island."

She pulled out her phone and started to call Charlotte, but then quickly changed her mind and pressed the button for Jay. Before he could say anything, she rushed her words. "Charlotte, I need you to do me a favor. I have a friend who needs a boat to get off the island."

"Hey, Robs. You called me, not Charlotte."

"I know, but he's responsible. Just needs to get to the mainland for some kind of emergency."

"Robs? You okay?"

"No, I don't think so. I'm here at the bungalow now. He's here with me." She turned to Freddy, stalling for time. "You'll need it only for the afternoon, right?"

Freddy circled nervously back and forth in the entrance to the house.

"I'm on my way." There was no mistaking the edge of urgency in Jay's voice.

The phone went dead, but she continued. "Yes, a powerboat would be fine. Yes. Okay, we'll head to the marina in about thirty minutes if you can have it ready then. And tell Ben, thanks." She slipped the phone into her pocket.

"So, I got you a powerboat. She said something about a center console." Robin wasn't sure what she was saying but just threw out some boating terms, hoping to buy time. "Do you know what kind of boat that is? Can you drive it? I hope it has gas in it for you." What else could she ramble about to stall? How long would it take Jay to get here?

"You're going to go with me." Freddy waggled his knife. "But the dog stays here."

"You don't need me."

"Yes, and you'll sweet talk them at the marina, too. The stupid sheriff has someone watching my boat, and watching the ferry, and I haven't been able to get away. But now, this will work. I'll hit the mainland and get out of this area. They'll never find me."

"You could just take the boat after you get it. You don't need me."

"I think it would be better if you stay with me until I know I'm safely away. That way you can't pull any tricks."

Unless, of course, they show up to the marina and no one knows anything about her calling for a boat...

She stalled some more. "I should lock Barney up in a room so he doesn't cause any trouble."

"Is that a closet?" He pointed to the closet in the corner.

She nodded.

"Put him in there."

"I can't put him in a closet."

He took a step forward. "Oh, yes, you can."

She walked over to the closet and opened

the door. "Come on, Barney." She tried to coax the dog.

He was having none of it. He stood where he was, his back taut, on alert, eyeing Freddy.

"Barney, come here."

"Get that dog locked up. Now."

"Barney, please." She pleaded with the dog, afraid of what Freddy might do.

Freddy took a step inside. "I'll deal with him."

"No, don't." She stepped away from the closet but saw a shadow cross her front window. "I've got him." She moved closer to Barney, trying to keep Freddy's attention on her.

She reached the dog and scooped him up right when Jay came crashing into the bungalow.

"What the—" Freddy whirled around but didn't have a chance.

Jay tackled him in one fell swoop, pinning him to the floor. The knife went ricocheting across the floor. Freddy wrestled beneath Jay's weight but couldn't get loose.

She heard a siren in the distance, coming closer.

"Robs, go outside. It's the sheriff."

She crossed to the doorway, keeping her eye

on Jay and the still-struggling Freddy. "Sheriff, over here."

Sheriff Dave rushed inside. "So, Jay. I see you did my work for me." The sheriff leaned over and handcuffed Freddy, then motioned for Jay to get up. "I know enough to apologize when I'm wrong about someone. And I was wrong about you."

Jay just nodded, then turned and walked over to her, pulling her into his arms. "You okay?" he whispered into her ear.

"I am now."

The sheriff took Freddy away and Jay turned to her. "What were you thinking coming here alone? I thought we agreed you'd stick close to me?"

"I just wanted to get a few things. It was broad daylight. I didn't think..."

He tilted her head up and he looked right into her eyes. "When you called. When I finally figured out you were in trouble and Freddy was here? I just about had a heart attack. Don't ever do that to me again. Promise me." He pulled her back into his arms and held her.

"I'm just glad you figured out what I was saying."

He pulled back and looked into her eyes.

"That's one thing about us, Robs. We can communicate with each other without saying the words." He stepped back for a moment. "But I want to get these words right. Say the right ones. When I thought he might take you away, that you might get hurt... that... I might lose you… Well, that can't happen. I need you. I *love* you."

She smiled at him. "And I love you, too."

He dropped to one knee and her mouth flew open wide.

"So, will you marry me, Robs? I want to spend every single day with you. The rest of our lives. I don't ever want to be apart."

"I—" Tears sprang to her eyes and she dropped down to the floor facing him. "Yes. I'd love to marry you."

"All right!" He jumped up, pulling her with him, and swirled her around the room in a dance. "You've made me the happiest man ever."

She laughed in joy. He finally put her down and gently wiped away her tears.

"Just you, me, Barney, and Sunny. A perfect family." She smiled, unable to contain her joy.

"So, one other thing." He cocked his head

to the side and gave that infectious grin. The one she could never say no to.

"Can we get married soon?"

"Yes, we can have a simple ceremony on the beach."

He sighed. "I wish we could just run off and get married."

"Why can't we?"

His mouth curled into a lazy grin. "Because Charlotte, Sara, and Lillian would kill us."

"Then let's invite them. And just a handful of people. Simple ceremony on the beach. Nothing fancy. I just want to be your wife. I feel like we've waited forever for this."

"When?" He looked at her doubtfully.

"Next weekend?" She grinned.

"Are you sure?"

"Never been so certain. Now that we've finally figured out we're in love, we should really do something about it."

"We should." He grinned back, then let out a whoop. "I'm marrying Robin Baker. Next week." He swung her around in a circle. "Or two weeks if we *have* to wait that long. I'm all generous like that."

CHAPTER 30

Zoe walked into Charming Inn and over to Lillian, standing at the reception desk. "Hey, Lillian. I got a message you wanted to see me?"

Lillian looked at her, a confused expression on her face. "What?"

"Uncle Noah said you had some things for me. Did I leave some of my stuff here when I left?"

"Zoe, I don't have any idea what you're talking about."

"Maybe we can clear things up." Mason and Gary strode up the desk.

"Gary, you're back." Lillian rushed from behind the desk, and Gary encircled her in an embrace. "I didn't know you were coming back today."

"Perks of a private jet." He grinned. "I'm back. Back to stay."

"But what about your job? The CEO position?"

"Lillian, you are my whole world. And I don't really want my world split in two places. So, I've come up with a plan." Gary turned to Mason. "But, for now, let's let these two talk."

Zoe stood staring at Mason. *Mason.* Back here on the island. Not anything she'd expected.

"Go ahead, son. Go talk to Zoe."

"Hey, you." Mason walked up and took her hand.

"Hi." Her voice was barely over a whisper.

"Can we talk?"

She nodded and he led her outside to a corner of the deck where they were alone. She turned to face him, and he took both her hands in him.

"I missed you," he said.

She'd missed him too. But seeing him like this, so soon, after she'd almost talked herself into believing she was getting used to him not being here...

He reached out and ran his fingers along her

cheek. "I've missed your smile, your laugh, even your messy ways."

A tentative, nervous laugh escaped her lips.

"Mostly, I missed just talking to you. Oh, and one more thing." He gave her his world-famous impish grin, and his one dimple deepened. "I missed kissing you."

He leaned in and kissed her. And again. Her world spun around as she kissed him back, clinging to him, hoping this wasn't all a dream.

He finally pulled back. "So, the thing is, I care about you. A lot. And how can we figure us out if I'm a six-hour flight away? I'll answer that. We can't. So... I'm going to stay here in Florida. Dad and I made plans. We have good managers in Seattle and good teams in Chicago and Minneapolis. We're national now on our projects, so we don't really need to be headquartered in Seattle. It appears we now own the majority stock in the company again, so we made a decision. We're going to run the company from Belle Island."

Her mind was reeling. Mason and Gary were going to be here? On the island?

"So, you'll only be a couple hours away and I can see you all the time." He paused, then said, "Right?"

"No." She looked at him and shook her head.

"No?" He frowned. "I thought… I'm sorry. I thought we were on the same page. That maybe you cared about me too."

"I do care about you."

"But then, why no?"

She reached out and touched his arm. "No, on the couple hours away."

His brow creased. "What do you mean?"

"Well, some things have changed since you left." She grinned. "I've moved back to the island."

"You have?" He grabbed both her hands. "You mean… you mean we're *both* going to be here on Belle Island?"

"Looks like it."

"I can't think of any better news." He broke into a grin.

"Ah, but there is so much to tell you."

"I'm all yours."

That sure sounded nice. All hers. She kicked off her shoes. "Come on, let's go for a walk on the beach."

He took off his shoes, rolled up the legs of his slacks and they headed to the beach.

"So, what's this you want to tell me?"

"Well first of all, will you be my date to Jay and Robin's wedding next weekend?"

He threw his head back and laughed. "Really? Well good for them."

He took her hand in his while they crossed the warm sand and stood beside the water looking out as the waves rolled toward them. "You know, Zoe. This island is kind of a magical place."

Contentment, intermingled with absolute happiness, washed through her as she leaned against him. "It really is, isn't it?"

CHAPTER 31

Robin stood on the edge of the beach at Charming Inn. Okay, she'd taken two weeks, not just one, but the wedding was planned and everything was perfect. They'd kept the wedding small, just like she'd wanted. Just a handful of friends.

She stood at the end of the aisle with Sara on one side of her and Charlotte on the other. She nodded to them and they walked her down the aisle toward Jay.

The setting sun threw sunbeams dancing across the waves. Birds winged through the sky above them. A gentle breeze kept the evening at the perfect temperature.

Charlotte leaned over and kissed her cheek before letting go of her arm. "Go to him. It's been five years. You two deserve your happiness."

And she let go of her friends and walked into the arms of the man she loved.

"You look beautiful," he whispered.

"You look..." She didn't even know the word to describe it. Handsome. Perfect. Charming. Welcoming. That was it. He looked like home.

They turned to the minister and said their vows. Then before she knew it, the minister was saying they were married.

Married.

She and Jay were married.

He leaned over and kissed her. Slowly. Thoroughly. She should care that everyone was watching, but she didn't. She circled her arms around his neck and clung to him.

"I love you, Jay."

"Love you right back, Mrs. Turner. With everything I have, everything I am."

And life fell into perfect place. She loved this man. With her whole heart. Her whole being. She'd found him. Her soulmate.

THEY FINALLY HAD a few moments alone at the reception and stood at the edge of the deck with the stars dancing above them. Music drifted across the deck, mixing with the gentle breeze. Lanterns cast gentle light around them. She stood quietly with him, watching the waves.

"It was a perfect night." She leaned against him.

"It was."

"I was kind of surprised you didn't show up in a t-shirt, though," she teased.

He grinned. "Oh, but of course I did." He unbuttoned his shirt and tugged it apart.

There, underneath the light blue dress shirt, was a gray t-shirt that said: Wishes do come true on Lighthouse Point.

DEAR READER,

I hope you enjoyed this addition to the Charming Inn series. Finally, Robin and Jay figured it all out! Now… what about Charlotte and Ben's wedding? Check out Charming Christmas - Book Seven - for a short holiday novel that brings the series to an end. (Well, at least for now. Never say never!)

And look for the Moonbeam Bay series. Coming in January 2021.

As always, thanks for reading my stories. I appreciate you all so much!

Kay

ALSO BY KAY CORRELL

COMFORT CROSSING ~ THE SERIES

The Shop on Main - Book One

The Memory Box - Book Two

The Christmas Cottage - A Holiday Novella (Book 2.5)

The Letter - Book Three

The Christmas Scarf - A Holiday Novella (Book 3.5)

The Magnolia Cafe - Book Four

The Unexpected Wedding - Book Five

The Wedding in the Grove (crossover short story between series - Josephine and Paul from The Letter.)

LIGHTHOUSE POINT ~ THE SERIES

Wish Upon a Shell - Book One

Wedding on the Beach - Book Two

Love at the Lighthouse - Book Three

Cottage near the Point - Book Four

Return to the Island - Book Five

Bungalow by the Bay - Book Six

CHARMING INN ~ Return to Lighthouse Point

One Simple Wish - Book One

Two of a Kind - Book Two

Three Little Things - Book Three

Four Short Weeks - Book Four

Five Years or So - Book Five

Six Hours Away - Book Six

Charming Christmas - Book Seven

SWEET RIVER ~ THE SERIES

A Dream to Believe in - Book One

A Memory to Cherish - Book Two

A Song to Remember - Book Three

A Time to Forgive - Book Four

A Summer of Secrets - Book Five

A Moment in the Moonlight - Book Six

INDIGO BAY ~ Save by getting Kay's complete collection of stories previously published separately in the multi-author Indigo Bay series. The three stories are all interconnected.

Sweet Days by the Bay

Or buy them separately:

Sweet Sunrise - Book Three

Sweet Holiday Memories - A short holiday story

Sweet Starlight - Book Nine

ABOUT THE AUTHOR

Kay writes sweet, heartwarming stories that are a cross between women's fiction and contemporary romance. She is known for her charming small towns, quirky townsfolk, and enduring strong friendships between the women in her books.

Kay lives in the Midwest of the U.S. and can often be found out and about with her camera, taking a myriad of photographs which she likes to incorporate into her book covers. When not lost in her writing or photography, she can be found spending time with her ever-supportive husband, knitting, or playing with her puppies —two cavaliers and one naughty but adorable Australian shepherd. Kay and her husband also love to travel. When it comes to vacation time, she is torn between a nice trip to the beach or the mountains—but the mountains only get considered in the summer—she swears she's allergic to snow.

Learn more about Kay and her books at kaycorrell.com

While you're there, sign up for her newsletter to hear about new releases, sales, and giveaways.

WHERE TO FIND ME:
kaycorrell.com
authorcontact@kaycorrell.com

Join my Facebook Reader Group. We have lots of fun and you'll hear about sales and new releases first!
https://www.facebook.com/groups/KayCorrell/

I love to hear from my readers. Feel free to contact me at authorcontact@kaycorrell.com

facebook.com/KayCorrellAuthor
instagram.com/kaycorrell
pinterest.com/kaycorrellauthor
amazon.com/author/kaycorrell
bookbub.com/authors/kay-correll

Made in the USA
Middletown, DE
30 October 2020